This book is dedicated to

the memory of my mother,

Charlotte Mae Walker.

She knew the importance of

letting her feet leave the ground.

And to Ben and Michael,

who keep reminding me

how it's done.

when I was eleven years old, my daddy was killed in a plane crash. I was pretty sure I had been the cause of it, but I hadn't told anybody. I had been carrying the secret around inside me, where it rested most days at the pit of my stomach. Other times, though, it would rise up and get stuck at the back of my throat like a sour ball of hard candy.

Then came the summer when I turned twelve. Three days into summer vacation and the stranger showed up at the door.

Now I didn't just open the door to the stranger when I heard the knock. I knew better than that. I looked through the front window. Well, it was a stranger. And he was very strange. He was short and a little on the pudgy side. He was all crinkly eyes and smiling and he had a gray mustache that covered a good part of his lower face. Next to him was a suit-case that looked like it had been dragged down the road behind a team of mules. I opened the big door but left the screen door locked. Not much protection, but better than nothing. If he tried to push his way in I figured I'd have time to run out the back. I have always been one to think about these things.

Mama was at the beauty shop, which was a real positive in my book, and if I do say so — my idea. It was the first good thing she had done for herself in a long time. I had talked her into getting a perm. Not a tight curl or anything like that, just a little body wave.

So, thanks to me, Mama was at the Clicking Clippers getting beautified. I had the whole afternoon to myself to start on the encyclopedias, which I felt would help me get caught up on what all I had missed in sixth grade. I hadn't missed sixth grade. I just had missed all the stuff I was supposed to learn in sixth grade. I was starting with M, as I didn't figure order was all that important in this case, and that was when I heard the knock at the door.

Petey, my dog, if he had been any kind of watchdog at all, should have barked to let me know that somebody was on the place. Usually, if he knew that I was inside the house, he'd be barking his head off to be let in. Petey was the kind of dog who was never satisfied being wherever he happened to be.

By nature I was not one who believed in a lot of hooey. Ask anybody, I have always had a good head on my shoulders. But that morning when I saw that little round man standing there on our porch wearing a red bill cap with the words PRAY HARD written on it, the thought popped in my head, *Your life will not be the same from this moment on.*

There I stood with nothing between me and the stranger but a flimsy screen door. Soon as he saw me he touched the brim of that PRAY HARD cap like he was saluting me and he said, "Why, Amelia Forrest, if you don't look just like your daddy! Where is that old rascal? You tell him Brother Mustard Seed is here just like he asked!"

He was going on and on, with no sign of stopping. Finally, I blurted out, "My daddy died in a plane crash last year." Then I closed the door on him with a big bang and flipped the dead bolt.

Well, that's when his crying jag started. I looked out the window and saw him sitting there on his sorry-looking old suitcase, which was kind of a dumb thing to do since we had perfectly good rocking chairs and a swing on the porch. Petey had finally come around, but instead of barking and threatening the stranger, he was trying to rest his head on the man's lap.

The guy's PRAY HARD cap fell off his head and rolled down the front steps into the yard. He must have been crying too hard to even notice. Petey jumped off the porch after the cap and started sniffing it.

Brother Mustard Seed! Who did he think he was kidding? I didn't believe *that* was his name for a minute! Where did he come from, anyway? He didn't drive up in any car, so that meant he had either hitched a ride or he walked. Probably walked, from the looks of his dusty shoes. He was wearing a pair of stiff-looking brown pants that were way too long and all bunched up around his ankles. They must have been brand-new. The way he was sitting gave me a good view of his backside, and I saw little white threads just above one of the pockets, showing where the tags had recently been yanked off. His shirt was pale yellow and still had fold marks on the sleeves and back. Like his pants, the shirt had "just bought" written all over it, except for two big sweat stains that reached out like dark half-moons from under both armpits. He sat there all hunched over, and every once in a while I would see his shoulders heave up and down. His tears splashed on the porch floor and soaked into the pine boards one fat drop at a time.

I figured that Mama would send this yahoo packing just as soon as she got back from the Clicking Clippers. How long did it take to get a perm, anyway? I paced around the living room a little and then I sat down. After a few minutes, I got up again and peeked out the window to make sure the crazy man was only sitting there and not trying to break in or anything.

If Oshun, my best friend, had been here, she

would have known what to do, but she was in Haiti with her mom and dad. They were studying voodoo, which I thought was a strange and maybe even dangerous thing to be studying. Every summer Oshun's parents would traipse about one place or another, do weird things, and then write about their adventures. The rest of the year they taught college students.

I could have been with them on this trip, but I turned down the offer. Oshun had practically begged me to go. Besides not paying much attention to my studies, I had stopped doing a lot of things I used to do with Oshun. We had been best friends since first grade, when Oshun and her parents moved to town. She claimed she wasn't the town-girl type and spent most of her time with her grandmother, who lived across the road from us. Oshun's grandma, Miss Waters, was our only neighbor in sight. Her place was kind of set off by a long front yard. Sometimes when Miss Waters sat in her porch swing she would wave and motion for me to come on over and have a visit, even when Oshun wasn't with her.

Oshun and I used to do almost everything together. One summer, a couple of years ago, we stuck adhesive Velcro strips down the right and left legs of our jeans. We stuck our legs together and walked around like that. We called our invention "Buddy Pants." My mom said we should make up a bunch and sell them at school. But we found that it was really hard to walk around in Buddy Pants. In fact, I almost broke my leg in them.

I missed Oshun and all the fun we used to have. This last year I mostly hung around the house and watched television when I had free time. It just seemed too weird to have fun, like I'd be ignoring everything that had happened.

I'd also been invited to the Summer Camp Bible School that the church puts on every year up at the lake. I'd attended that Bible School camp every year that I could remember. I decided I'd made enough glued-on macaroni pictures of holy scenes to last a lifetime. Besides, I wasn't all that close with the church kids anymore, and Mama hadn't insisted that I go, so

I let that bus pass right by me. I wasn't dumb, I knew why the church people and Oshun's family were trying to get me to do things with them, but I had my own ideas about what would be good for me.

Mama had said, "If you want to go with them, Amelia, then you should go." Whether she would admit it or not, though, Mama needed my help. If you had asked me, I think she was relieved when I turned down the offers. I bet she would have worried herself sick over me down there in Haiti studying voodoo. I mean, it wasn't like they were inviting me on a trip to Disney World or someplace like that. Oshun's parents didn't do those kinds of vacations.

A couple of summers ago Oshun's folks got themselves lowered into the Atlantic in a shark-proof cage, dangled raw meat between the bars until the sharks started to attack, then took pictures. Oshun brought back matching shark's tooth necklaces for us. This trip she planned to find a voodoo doll that looked like Mr. Pascal, our P.E. teacher. Then we'd see how many laps around the track he'd make us run!

Oshun said we should always wear our shark's tooth necklaces for good luck and protection. I didn't really believe in the good luck and protection part; I just thought it was pretty neat to wear a tooth that had come out of a shark's mouth. Oshun believed in it, though. She believed in a lot of stuff, like ghosts, and fortune-telling, and charms — at least she said she did. With Oshun, you couldn't always tell the difference between what she really believed and what she just *wanted* to believe. It was like she made it up as she went along and it was always changing.

That was a lot different from people who believed in the Bible, for instance. There was a book full of rules about how to live — no ifs, ands, or buts. And it was loaded with stories about what happened to people when they followed the rules and when they didn't. At least I guessed that's what it was mostly about. And as far as I knew, the rules never changed and hadn't changed since they were first written on those two big stones. Not like I had ever read the Bible from cover to cover or anything, but I did know parts of it. And I doubted there was anything in there about how wearing a shark's tooth on a string around your neck would protect you from nuts who showed up and sat on your front porch.

I sat there near the door and held the shark's tooth, anyway. Not because I thought it would help me, but just because I liked the way it felt in my hand. I listened to the crying and the weird mumbling coming from the front porch. Finally, I heard Mama's car crunch the gravel in the driveway. Finally!

The woman who stepped out of the car was definitely not the same mother I had sent off to the beauty shop that morning. This woman had orangey-red hair, and it curled around her head in what I thought was a most unflattering style. She was wearing her usual Saturday running-errands outfit, which was a red sweat suit. She stood there next to her car looking up at the crybaby on the front porch, and I thought to myself, *My mama looks just like a fireplug.*

"Is that you, Brother Mustard Seed?" Mama asked the man.

How in the Sam Hill did she know his name?

What was going on here, and why did I feel like the day was just swallowing me up whole?

Next thing I knew, the big baby was bouncing off the porch and right into my mama's arms! She was hugging him, and he was blubbering and carrying on. Crying and saying, "Oh, Mrs. Forrest, I didn't know! I didn't know!"

My mama just kept patting him on the back, saying, "It's okay. Cry and get it all out." Personally I didn't see how he had any left in him to get out, since it seemed like he'd been letting it all out for the last hour or so right there on the front porch.

"I'm okay," he said, and then he pulled a bandanna out of his front pocket and blew his nose. I swear you could have heard that foghorn all the way over to Miss Waters's house.

So one minute the big crybaby was perched out there on top of that broken-down old suitcase and then the next minute he was in our house, sitting on our sofa. Well, wouldn't you know it, he got one glimpse of that picture of Daddy up on the fireplace mantel and he started in again. Mama sat next to him and rubbed little circles on his back while he cried, which was what she always did to me when I cried or vomited. It was the same treatment. She reached into her pocket and pulled out a tissue for him, as that bandanna of his must have been soaked through. One thing about Mama, she could always come up with a tissue when you needed one.

After what seemed like a really long time, he finally stopped crying. His face was red, and that nasty old mustache of his was wet from tears and maybe even snot.

"You feel like talking now?" Mama asked him.

He nodded and looked at me. I thought he might tune up and cry again, but he didn't. He said, "Amelia Forrest, you're the spitting image of your daddy, do you know that?"

I didn't say anything. I felt like it was one of those questions that didn't require an answer. But he was right. I looked at Daddy's picture on the mantel. We both had sandy blond hair and blue eyes. Mama's hair was brown; well, it used to be brown before she went off to the Clicking Clippers that morning. Both me and Daddy had long, thin faces. In fact, both of us were what you might call skinny all over. I was going to be tall like Daddy, too. I could tell already. I was the tallest girl in my sixth-grade class last year. I think my feet would have finally reached the rudder pedals. I'm pretty sure that this would have been the summer that I got to fly the plane with my feet actually touching the pedals — something I'd always wanted to do.

Mama was short and she had put on a lot of weight since Daddy died. It seemed like she was eating something all the time, even though she didn't cook as much as she used to. Instead, she would bring in sacks full of those little Dazy Dan hamburgers and French fries. Sometimes we'd eat Dazy Dans for three or four days in a row. Daddy had hated Dazy Dans. He called them "gut bombs."

Right before school vacation started I saw a television commercial where a real attractive man said, "Good mental health, you owe it to yourself and the ones you love!" I decided he was right. Mama and me could use a dose of good mental health. It was time I started taking care of things like Daddy had always asked me to do whenever he went away. I had made up my mind that this summer was going to be a time for me and Mama to get back in shape — to get our acts together, I guess you could say. I would see to it that Mama got off the junk food, and I'd get her to start caring about the way her hair looked again. For my own improvement, I was going to catch up on all the stuff that I hadn't paid attention to in sixth grade. And when school started again I fully intended to be a better friend to Oshun and to stop watching so much television.

But talk about watching your plans fly out the window! Somehow I knew that this surprise visit had all the potential of turning into more than just an afternoon distraction. Two unexpected things in one day! Between Mama's new dye job and this drop-in visitor, it was like having your train derail right before your very eyes. One minute you were just chugging along making good time, and the next thing you knew your cars were bent, twisted, and piled up on both sides of the track. There my new redheaded Mama sat next to that little moon-eyed man who was mopping up his face with a damp bandanna. From head to toe, Mama looked like a firecracker that was about to go off.

Once Brother Mustard Seed got himself sort of straightened out, Mama began to give him the details about my daddy's GOD DELIVERS mission. The one that turned out to be his last. He sat there listening, just listening, as Mama talked about it. She told it like it was something she'd read about in the newspaper. It was about time for me to leave the room. Every time she told the story I would always leave before she got to the part when she would say, "And they never found out what caused the crash. I don't guess we'll ever know."

Brother Mustard Seed shook his head after every pause in Mama's story. I was standing up to leave when the screen door rattled the way it did when a wind picked up. We all looked toward the door at the same time, like we expected somebody to come walking on in there.

"Amelia, run out to the car and see if I rolled up the windows. I think a storm's coming."

Well, that gave me just the excuse I needed. I stepped out onto the porch as I heard her say, "They found his plane scattered all up and down the side of a mountain over in eastern Kentucky."

I had always wondered about that mountain, wondered if it had a name like some mountains do. I figured it didn't, since somebody would most likely have called it by its name if it had one. I knew it wouldn't have made any kind of difference, but it really bothered me that the mountain wasn't named anything. It didn't seem fair. Either all mountains should get names or none of them should. My daddy's mountain deserved a name as much as Mount Everest or any other mountain.

mama was right about the storm. The sky had turned a dark gray. The clouds were rolling and building into the kind of storm that Daddy called a toad-stringer, meaning the storm would be so fierce that it would string toads all up and down the road, even though I had never actually seen that happen myself.

I rolled up the windows and started back to the house when the clouds split open and the rain fell out like you'd turned over a bucket. I ran to the porch with thunder banging behind me like it was the devil on my tail.

That man's red PRAY HARD cap was sticking out a little bit from under the porch where Petey had dragged it. I jumped down there real quick and snatched up the cap before it got soaked. And then, for some reason, I hid it behind a big pot of geraniums on the porch before I went back in the house.

There I found the man shaking his head back and

forth and he was saying, "It was sort of like a dream, but I was awake. It was a vision, is what it was — a dog-gone, real-as-life vision of your husband, Mrs. Forrest. He stood right before my very eyes as sure as I'm sitting here."

The rain made a thunderous roar as it hit the porch roof, but I still heard him loud and clear. The next thing I knew, a flash of lightning seemed to come right into the room with us. I felt the hairs on my arm rise. I remembered a television special I saw once called *Close Brushes with Death*, where a man said his arm hairs stood up right before he got struck by lightning. I dropped to the floor and covered up my ears. Petey, who didn't like storms one bit, had followed me inside. He started howling when I hit the deck. Maybe he thought I had been struck.

Mama ran over to me and said, "Good Lord, Amelia, what was THAT all about?"

"She tripped over the dog, ma'am," Brother Mustard Seed said.

I started to sit up once I realized I hadn't been

struck. "I didn't trip," I said. "I dropped to the ground on purpose. It felt like the lightning came right in."

"That was a close one, Mrs. Forrest," Brother Mustard Seed put in.

Mama looked toward the window. The sky had turned dark as night, and the wind howled around the corner of the house like a banshee. "I think it's time to get to the basement," she said. Then she reached down and helped pull me to my feet.

When I thought about it later, I wasn't sure if I had covered my ears to drown out the sound of the storm or to keep from hearing what Brother Mustard Seed was telling Mama about seeing Daddy in a vision.

We sat out the rest of the storm in the basement. Petey yelped every time there was another crack of thunder and wouldn't leave Brother Mustard Seed's side. Why wasn't Petey suspicious of this guy? It seemed like he had just accepted him lock, stock, and barrel.

We listened to the weather guy on the little radio we had down there just for such purposes. Weather Bill's voice crackled through: "No tornadoes so far, but I'll keep you folks posted. Be sure and call in if you spot one out your way!"

"Just a summer storm," Mama said. "It'll pass soon enough." Then she turned the volume down until Weather Bill's voice could barely be heard above the noise of the storm. "Go on, Brother Mustard Seed, tell us more about this vision you had."

"Jed Forrest had been on my mind a lot lately. One thing that bothered me was that he hadn't been out to the prison in some time. He used to drop in every once in a while to say hello. But he didn't show up at Christmas. Then along came spring and summer and I figured he was busy with his crop dusting. I guessed I'd see him again in the fall."

"I'm so sorry, I should have let you know — " Mama began, but he cut her off.

"No, ma'am, I understand, I just wanted you to know that he'd been on my mind. So when I had that vision I figured that maybe I'd brought it on myself."

"Well, I should have let you know," Mama said again. It seemed to me like Mama had been full of *should haves* since the accident. *We should have gone to church last Sunday. I should have made a good supper for us tonight. I should have that field mowed. You should have studied harder, Amelia.* That was one of the reasons I intended to get both Mama and me back on track. I was getting tired of hearing all of her *should haves*.

Brother Mustard Seed went on with his story. I noticed that Mama's hand had gone up to those new red curls of hers, and while she listened, she sort of pulled at them, sort of uncurled them, and then let them snap back in place.

"I was sitting at the edge of the basketball court in the prison yard. Not playing — I never got picked due to my size — but they let me keep score because I'm honest. It was a slow game, and my mind was drifting off a little bit. Now there was a big old oak tree just left of the picnic tables, and I happened to be looking up that way. I saw a bright ball of light sort of settle itself up near the top branches. *What's that?* I asked myself, and then I squinted to get a better look. That ball of light sort of floated down out of the tree and stretched itself out into a column right in front of me. I looked around to see if the guys playing ball could see what I was seeing. But the game was going on as usual, and I found I didn't even have a voice to say, 'Hey, would you look at this!' Next thing I knew, in place of the light, was Brother Jed Forrest. He looked right at me, felt like he was looking right *through* to my insides! He said, 'Go to my family. They need your help.'"

Outside, the rain hit the ground in heavy, dirt-pounding buckets. For a minute the rain and the low grumble of thunder were the only sounds heard in the basement.

Then Brother Mustard Seed clapped his hands and stamped his foot. Both Mama and me jumped, and she reached out for my hand. Petey barked once but then settled right back down where he'd been lying next to Brother Mustard Seed's foot.

"Poof!" Brother Mustard Seed hollered out above the storm. "And Brother Jed was gone! Just that quick. No more light, no more vision, no nothing!"

I guess he noticed the jumping and the barking, because he asked us, "Is this bothering you? I'll quit right now if you want me to."

Mama looked at me and said, "You okay, Amelia?"

I just nodded. I wouldn't exactly say I was okay, though. My daddy had been gone a year, and hearing this was sort of like hearing that he'd been spotted somewhere off in another town.

"Go on, Brother Mustard Seed," Mama said at last. "We're all right." But she pulled me up to her a little tighter. The chemical scent of hair dye around Mama's head made my eyes burn. I hoped they didn't get the wrong idea and think I was blinking back tears because of what this man was telling us.

Brother Mustard Seed started back in with the story where he had left off.

"Well, now, I looked back up to the top of the oak tree, but all I saw was a big flock of blackbirds. Big old birds, flapping their wings and squawking and shaking the branches. Then the birds flew off. Next thing I know, the ballplayers are yelling at me, 'What's the score, Mustard Seed?' and I had to tell them I didn't know. They didn't like that."

He shook his head back and forth and rubbed his big hands together like he was trying to rub out stains or something. I guess his hands were dry, because as he rubbed them, they made scratchy sounds.

"Ma'am, I'm sorry. I don't know what to make of any of this. I don't know why I'm here, except to say that I felt your husband called me. I'm just here to answer the call, if that makes any sense."

"You didn't escape from jail, did you?" Mama asked.

Good question, I thought, and was so proud of my mama for thinking of it. After all, an ex-convict is one thing, but an *escaped* convict is another thing altogether.

"Well, now, the Lord works in mysterious ways, Mrs. Forrest. I knew that just because I had a vision that said, 'Go,' I couldn't sashay out of the prison and go. I had five more years on my sentence! I felt real peculiar knowing I had to do something but not knowing how I was supposed to go about doing it. I stewed about it all night long — prayed, read the Bible. Then, the very next day, I got called into the warden's office. There was a legal fellow there. He told me that due to one thing or another, plus the fact that I got some time off for good behavior after I found the Lord, my sentence had been reduced. They turned me loose the next day."

"I'm . . . well, I'm just not sure I know what any of this means — do you?" Mama asked. I didn't know who the question was for, since she wasn't looking at me or at Brother Mustard Seed. I guess it didn't make any difference, anyway, because nobody answered.

For a while they talked about other things. Things that had nothing to do with my daddy or prisons or bright lights and dark birds in oak trees. Some of it I listened to and some of it I tuned out. I concentrated instead on the deep rumbles of thunder and the soothing voice of Weather Bill saying that the storm was passing and that everything was going to be okay.

ꟿꭹ daddy crashed his plane while he was flying one of his GOD DELIVERS missions for the church. He was taking food and supplies to some people who had been flooded out of their homes over in the eastern part of Kentucky. Several families were stranded on a ridge up in the mountains until the water let down. It seemed like between fires, floods, tornadoes, or drought, there was always one disaster or another going on over there.

Every time there was another act of God, all the church people would turn out and load up my daddy's crop-dusting plane with canned goods and off he'd go. I always hoped that at least one of those poor people had the good sense to take along a can opener before they got run out of their houses.

There wasn't much left of the plane after the rescuers found it. I heard somebody tell Mama that the plane looked like a toy that had been flung against the side of the mountain by an angry child. I pictured God as a spoiled little boy who got mad because he didn't get his way about something and threw the first thing he got his hands on. But in my heart I knew better. I knew that this time, anyway, God didn't have a thing to do with the disaster. It was me and the stupid thing I did that morning that caused my daddy's plane to crash.

I halfway expected an investigator to show up at our door and tell Mama he had found evidence that would prove it was my fault. But all they ever said was that the cause of the crash was undetermined.

I meant to tell Mama, especially in the beginning, when I thought it would be better for her to hear it from me than from a stranger. Then I'd look at her teary eyes and realize that I didn't even know how to start. It seemed like I'd just be upsetting her more, so I decided to wait for a while. And then the longer I didn't tell her, the easier it got to hold it in. Before I knew what had happened, the secret just took root inside me.

I almost told Miss Waters once. We were sitting at her kitchen table working a jigsaw puzzle together. I thought about telling her and tried to think of what words I'd say first, to imagine what she would say back to me. But in the end I just choked and couldn't do it.

Right after we first got the news it seemed like I couldn't make any connection between the bustle going on around me and the fact that Daddy and his plane were not coming back. People came over in droves. All the neighbors and the church people brought trays full of ham and cheese, plates full of deviled eggs, and bowls full of every color Jell-O salad you can imagine. Cakes and pies covered every flat surface in the house.

It felt like Daddy might come waltzing into the room any minute, look around at all the food and people, and say, "Whoop-de-doo! What a party!" He'd pick me up and holler, "Show us your wings, Amelia." And then he'd buzz me around like an airplane.

We used to play the airplane game a long time ago — when I was about five or six years old. I had gotten too big to be flown around like that. But still, it seemed like that's what I was waiting for. It was too bad that we couldn't have some ceremony for the "last time" of things. Who knew that the last time we played the airplane game it would be our last? I guess we just laughed and flew and buzzed around like there would always be a next time and another next time.

It made me start thinking about the "last time" of things that I could remember. I would always remember the last time Daddy kissed me good night, because it was the night before the plane crash.

And I'd always remember the last joke he played on me — it was also the night before the plane crash.

He had a plastic pop-up toy that looked like a little green monster on a spring. You could push the monster down and two suction cups would hold it together until all of a sudden — you never knew when — *POP!* The suction cups would release and the monster would fly straight up in the air with a loud *pop* and whistle, scaring the dickens out of you. The last night he tucked me in bed he put the green monster popper on the floor next to my bed, but of course I didn't know it.

I was about half asleep when the thing went off. I jumped straight up in bed and screamed. Then I heard him laughing outside my door. He came in and found the little monster popper across the room where it had landed.

"See there, Amelia, it was just a joke! It's a toy!" He showed me how it worked.

Mama was with him and she said, "Lord, Jed, you're going to turn the child into a nervous wreck!"

"Aww, come on, she loved it. That was a good one, wasn't it, Amelia?"

Getting woke up so fast had made my heart race, and I felt cranky.

"I didn't like it one bit, Daddy. Mama's right, you're turning me into a nervous wreck."

"Now, now, Amelia! You're one of the toughest cookies I know. You're not turning into a nervous Nellie, are you?"

And then he started singsonging, "Nervous Nellie, nervous Nellie, my Amelia's a nervous Nellie!"

He was prancing around the room and acting so silly that I laughed a little bit even though I didn't want to. But then I told him that he would be sorry because I would get him back good.

"Oooooh!" he said. "I'm shaking in my boots, nervous Nellie. Here's the big old bad monster that scared my nervous Nellie!"

He put the toy on the table next to my bed so that I could see that it was not spring-loaded and there was no danger of it going off again.

He blew me a kiss from the door, but I didn't even pretend to catch it like I usually did. Instead, I yelled back, "You're gonna be sorry!"

I saved the last note I got from him, which I found on the refrigerator the morning that he left.

Amelia,

I'll see you tonight. Keep the runway clear!

Daddy

P.S. You are no NERVOUS NELLIE. You're my brave Amelia, and I love you very much.

"Keep the runway clear" was his way of saying, "Take care of things while I'm gone." We had a grass landing strip next to our house. It was my job to help him keep the sticks and other debris picked up so that he would have a safe and smooth landing. But it meant more than that, too. It also meant, "Look after your mama." "Feed the dog." That sort of thing.

For a long time after the crash I would go out and pick up sticks and trash and other stuff that had blown over and cluttered up the place. But then I just stopped. It wasn't long until it looked like any other field you might see if you drove down our road. Besides sticks and stuff like that there were also cans and other junk all over the place. I guess we had a lot of litterbugs living around here.

Then one day I noticed the weeds growing high in the field and I realized that Mama had stopped paying the Ray brothers to come mow it.

There was a time when Mama and me would get out old photo albums and look at our pictures. Every few weeks or so we'd go to the cemetery to change the flowers on Daddy's grave. We'd talk about him and cry together, and then we'd laugh about the funny things he used to do. Mama always made sure I called Daddy's relations from time to time to say hello and send birthday cards and all. But then we sort of stopped doing it — all of it. We stopped keeping the field mowed. We stopped looking at our photo albums. We stopped going to church. We stopped everything. It was like there had been some clock keeping us both going, and then it just finally wound down and quit ticking.

I can't say for sure when it all started to change. Mama was busy with her job as the secretary at the high school, and I was busy being in sixth grade even though you couldn't tell it by my report card. I guess you could say that I was busy just showing up every day and maybe that's how it was for Mama, too. It felt like one big effort just to get out of bed every morning. I didn't care about being with my friends, even though Oshun and some of the others really tried. I got lots of invitations for sleepovers and parties, but I said no to every one of them.

On the day of the funeral, a churchwoman said to me, "Amelia, we are surely going to miss your daddy. But just know, honey, that the Lord must have needed him for some important work in heaven." I had to bite my tongue to keep from smarting off to that old biddy. That morning, when Mama had been helping me with my hair, she had said almost the same words about Jesus needing Daddy in heaven and it all being a part of God's plan. I guess it was some sort of standard church excuse. I said, "We need him more." Mama paused with the hairbrush a few inches above my head. Her words were almost too soft to hear, but

I was looking at her face in the mirror and saw her lips move. She said, "I know."

A few weeks later I got up in the night to get a drink of water. Mama was at the kitchen table with a bunch of papers spread out and a calculator in front of her. "Amelia," she said to me, "there's no rhyme or reason to anything in this world. You've gotta be ready for *anything* that could happen." Of course, that's something I had already figured out.

I wished I could tell her what I had done the morning that Daddy left on his last GOD DELIVERS mission, but I didn't know how. I guess I was a coward for not telling. I was ashamed for anybody to know what had happened. I was scared, too. What would Mama think about me? What would other people say if they found out? Sometimes I thought I might feel better if I told her, but I couldn't bring myself to do it. I got really good at putting it out of my head. I would only think about the fun we had with Daddy. I would go over everything that was good about our lives until that last day and then I would cut my thinking off. It got easier to do, believe it or not.

Sometimes Daddy felt like a real person to me, but more and more he had started to seem like a character I'd read about in a book or seen on television. That's when I started writing down everything I could remember about him in a notebook.

I have things like:

I remember that Daddy's hair smelled like leather when he came back from flying, because he used to wear that leather cap with the wings on the front.

And another good one is this:

I remember one time when Daddy tried to fix his watch, but I guess he decided it was hopeless. He started swinging it back and forth in front of my face and he said, "Come here, Amelia, watch

this." Then he opened the back door and threw
the watch across the yard and said, "My how time
flies!" It took me a minute to get it, but when I did
I laughed my head off.

The reason I started my memory book was because I figured that if I wrote down everything I could remember about him, he might still be like a character in a book to me, but at least it would be *my* book.

But I have other stuff in my book besides memories. I have a lot of pages filled with the same three-word sentence written over and over as many times as I could get it on the page, both front and back.

I am sorry. I am sorry. I am sorry. I am sorry. I
am sorry. I am sorry. I am sorry. I am sorry. I am
sorry. I am sorry. I am sorry. I am sorry. I am
sorry. I am sorry. I am sorry. I am sorry. I am
sorry. I am sorry.

When I started having the dream, I wrote that down, too. Every time I had the dream I would write it in my book, and it was always the same.

I can see my daddy's plane, even though it is night. It looks like a white moth flying in a circle high above the trees. I hear a popping sound and I know that he's in trouble. I also know that the only way he can pullout of it is to lighten the load and then try to find a place to land. I start yelling, "Throw out the canned goods!" I see cans of beans, yams, and tuna tumble out of the plane. I start to run to get away from them because I think they are going to fall on my head. After a while I stop running. I'm in a wide-open field and I think what a great place it is for my daddy to land the plane. But when I look up I see that now the plane is so light, it begins to float up and up like a helium balloon. Then, even though he is very high, I can see my daddy's face. He gives me a funny shrug, like he's trying to say, "Well, what do you know about this?!" The plane is rising higher and higher until finally it is nothing more than a white speck, smaller than all the stars around it. I keep my eyes focused on the speck, thinking that as long as I can see it, I can bring it back down, but then I blink. Just like that, I blink. I can't help it. And he's gone.

While we waited out the thunderstorm in the basement, Mama told me how she and Daddy first got to know Brother Mustard Seed.

"Back when you were a little baby, me and your daddy used to go over to the Stinson Correctional Facility with a church mission group that your daddy had started. We'd give out Bibles, snacks, magazines — whatever they needed. We were there to help out, to visit with the ones who didn't have visitors and to pray with the ones who wanted to pray."

"You mean the prison, right?" I asked. I knew that the Stinson Correctional Facility was a prison, but for some reason I wanted her to say it.

That's when Brother Mustard Seed started putting in his two cents' worth.

"It was a prison, Amelia. You're right about that. A fancy name didn't change the fact that it was still a prison. My name used to be J. E. Abernathy, and I did some bad things. That old Stinson Correctional Facility wasn't correcting a thing in me. It just made me meaner. But, thanks to your daddy, I gave my life to the Lord, and I changed my name to remind me that the old J. E. Abernathy died and was reborn. 'Mustard Seed' reminds me of my faith. Keeps me going straight. 'If ye have faith as a grain of mustard seed . . . nothing shall be impossible unto you' — Matthew, chapter seventeen, verse twenty."

I didn't need a Bible lesson, I was thinking to myself. I'd had all the Bible lessons I needed, thank you very much. Back when Daddy was alive we were in church every time the door was open. I liked how it used to feel to sit in between Mama and Daddy, I liked singing most of the songs, and I liked the lemon furniture polish smell that the church always had on Sunday mornings. But I thought the Bible was too hard to read and probably way over my reading level. Not that kids actually had to read the Bible. Instead, we got little Sunday school booklets full of lessons about kids who never acted like any kids I'd ever known. At least the Bible had a few adventure stories about the people who lived way back then. The stories in our booklets always seemed to be about one goody-goody kid and one really bad kid and in the end the bad kid learned a valuable lesson and turned into a goody-goody kid. Most kids I knew were a lot more average than that.

And as far as that verse about the mustard seed? Well, it happened to be one I'd memorized. Even though I had learned to say it by heart, I didn't know what it meant, because it seemed to me that lots of things were impossible. So I asked Miss Page, my Sunday school teacher, about it, and she said, "Faith can move mountains, Amelia." But she couldn't tell me how, and I finally had to let it go without getting a satisfactory answer.

I didn't feel like arguing with this man about mustard seeds or mountain-moving. I decided we needed to get to the meat of the prison matter. I asked him, "What did you do, anyway? What landed you in prison in the first place?"

He looked at Mama like he needed her permission to go on with the story. She shrugged her shoulders. I guess he decided it was okay to tell me about whatever he did to get himself hauled off to jail.

"I used to park cars for a living, up in Louisville at a real fancy hotel right by the river. It was so fancy that my uniform was a tuxedo and white gloves. Oh, you should have seen the cars those folks would drive up in! Well, I started saving, saving every dime I could get hold of, to get my own car someday. One evening I was parking a long, dark beauty of a car, and I happened to catch sight of my reflection in the rearview mirror. I thought, *Well, now, don't I look good in this here automobile!* How long did I think I was going to have to work to save enough money to own a car that fine? I figured it wasn't fair that some folks had enough money to buy those big, beautiful automobiles with real leather seats and other folks, like me, had to park them. The next thing I know I'm out on Interstate sixty-five and the blue lights are flashing behind me."

"You stole the car? Just like that? You just drove away in it?" I asked. I didn't think he looked much like a car thief. He didn't have that thug look about him — but, I guess, you never could tell.

"I stole the car and the only thing I was sorry for was being dumb enough to get caught. I swore that as soon as I was out of prison I'd steal me another one. I'd just be smarter the next time. If it hadn't been for your daddy coming along to prison when he did, I'd a still been thinking about the life of crime I'd picked out for myself."

I think that Mama wanted him to stop talking about the prison part. She jumped in and sort of summed up the rest. Said that he found the Lord after listening to my daddy's talk one day at the prison, started reading the Bible all the time, and told everybody there that he wanted to be called Brother Mustard Seed from then on out. I didn't know how well this went over with the other inmates, and Mama didn't say.

After a while the church stopped the prison

mission and went on to other things, like the GOD DELIVERS mission. But Daddy would still drop by from time to time, to see how the prisoners were doing and take them treats and knickknacks. Brother Mustard Seed said he always made sure he had a chance to shake his hand and thank him all over again for the work that he was doing.

"Your daddy would reach out and give me a big ol' hug. Then he'd say, 'Don't thank me, I'm just a crop duster!'"

It got real quiet in the basement after that. The storm had ended, and Mama switched off Weather Bill's radio show. I sat there and thought, *Yep, that sounds just like something Daddy would say.*

And then I remembered why Brother Mustard Seed was sitting there in the basement with us. He said Daddy had appeared to him in a vision and told him to come to us. But why was he really here? Maybe this man was some kind of a con artist. I saw a report on television once about con artists who showed up and took you for a ride. One old widow woman on television lost her whole life's savings because a couple of men talked her into letting them put a new roof on her house. They climbed up on top and then came down and said her roof was full of holes. She wrote them out a check for thousands of dollars, and off they went to town to get her some new roof shingles. Well, she never saw them or her money again.

Maybe this man was sort of homeless or something and thought that my daddy was a soft touch and would let him stay here. He hadn't even known about the plane crash when he showed up at the door. Maybe he conjured up the story about the vision while he was sitting out there on the front porch pretending to cry. On the other hand, if that had been pretend-crying, the man should win an Oscar. I finally decided I couldn't figure out what he was up to, but I could say for certain that I didn't get a good feeling about having him show up like he did — especially with a suitcase.

I told Mama that I thought I'd go check on Miss

Waters to see if she made it through the storm all right. I had promised Oshun and her family that I'd look after Miss Waters while they were away even though Oshun's grandmother didn't really need looking after. I just liked visiting her. I hoped that our visitor would be gone by the time I got back, so I said my proper good-byes to him, thinking that he'd take the hint.

Holding out my hand, I said, "Well, it was nice to meet you. You have a good trip, now."

He grabbed my hand and started pumping it up and down. His palm felt hot and dry. "Oh, Amelia Forrest, you are just like your daddy, you are!" I could see tears welling up in his eyes again, so I turned on a dime and got out of there.

Mama excused herself and followed me out the door, leaving Brother Mustard Seed in the house with all our valuables, which didn't seem like such a good idea. "Amelia, are you okay? I know that J. E. — er, I mean Brother Mustard Seed — is a little out of the ordinary. But he means well, he really does. Your daddy thought an awful lot of him."

"I guess so, Mama. I just get a creepy feeling from him — you know, with the vision and all that. Plus the fact that he just got out of *prison*."

Mama gave me a little kiss on the forehead and said, "Let's just see what he wants. That's all, okay? We'll just see what brought him out here." Then she turned around and went back in the house.

I wanted to say, "His squatty little legs brought him here and his squatty little legs better take him back again." But I didn't say it because it sounded fresh-mouthed. And one thing Mama didn't like was a fresh-mouth.

As I was walking over to see Miss Waters, I wondered what this so-called Brother Mustard Seed's plans were. How was he going to get to wherever he meant to go? Maybe he would walk back to town and take a bus or something. Or maybe he would *steal* another car — maybe *our car*. Or more than likely he would talk Mama into giving him a ride to town. But that was not my problem. I didn't care how he got out, as long as he got out soon.

"Amelia, you look like a drowned rat!" Miss Waters said to me when I walked into her kitchen.

Even though I had lived across the road from Miss Waters my entire life, she always looked surprised to see me. But I knew that it wasn't because she was really surprised; it was because of her eyebrows. She would pluck out her real eyebrows and draw in new ones. Oshun told me one time that her grandmother was born without eyebrows, but I didn't believe that. In fact, I saw her sitting on her porch once just plucking away. The ones that she drew in always seemed a little too high on her forehead, and I think that's what gave her that constant surprised look.

"Still raining?" she asked me.

"Just a drizzle," I said. But I noticed that I was leaving a little puddle on her kitchen floor.

Miss Waters started cutting two big pieces of

lemon cake for us. We sat at the table and did a little small talking while we ate. I told her I'd sent a letter to Oshun down in Haiti and that I hoped she'd write back to me.

Then she said, "Amelia, what's troubling you, girl?"

Just like that. Miss Waters always seemed to know when something was going on — sometimes even when you didn't. Oshun said her grandmother had a special way of seeing, like special powers or something, but I didn't know about that. It just seemed to me like she was really smart.

"Come on, let's go out and dry off the porch swing. I love that fresh, after-a-rain smell, don't you? Then, if you want to, you can tell me what's on your mind." She tossed me a dish towel, and we headed out to her front porch.

As I was drying off the slats in the porch swing, I jumped right in and started telling her about the crazy crybaby.

"Miss Waters, there's a man, an ex-convict, at our

house and he says that he had a vision of Daddy while sitting out in the prison yard a few days ago."

"A vision? Is that right?"

"He says my daddy appeared to him and said something like, 'Go to my family. They need your help.'"

I started to go on with the story, but Miss Waters interrupted me and asked, "Well, is the man right, Amelia? Do you think you and your mama need help?"

What was she asking me that for? It didn't have a thing to do with what I was telling her. I mean, I'm not saying we didn't need help. For the last year it seemed like our lives had been spinning around and around. Sometimes it felt like I would get dizzy from it all and just fall down. And I believe the same thing was happening to Mama even though she wouldn't talk about it. I guess in a way we did need help. But I had big plans for our summer of improvement. That's all we needed, and I knew I could take care of it. What we didn't need was some car-stealing ex-con having visions, coming around to complicate things for us. Things would be okay, I knew, as soon as he was gone.

"Mama and me are doing just fine," I said to Miss Waters. "And even if we did need help, it wouldn't be from somebody who calls himself Brother Mustard Seed. I think he's a lunatic."

Miss Waters laughed and patted my hand. "Go on with your story, Amelia. What else did this fellow say?"

I told her everything, just the way Brother Mustard Seed had told it in the basement.

I saw Miss Waters look over at the grass strip where Daddy used to land his plane. The hard rain had flattened out the weeds until it almost looked like a runway ready for business. I knew that as soon as the sun came out, the weeds would spring right back up again.

"Your daddy was a good man, Amelia. He was always helping out folks in one way or another. Maybe you and your mama are doing just fine, but maybe your daddy sees something different from where he is.

Do you believe that your daddy might have appeared to this man in a vision? Do you think that's possible?"

It seemed to me that Miss Waters had a lot of questions but not many answers, which was not like her. I had plenty of questions and could have done with a few answers myself. In this situation it didn't seem like Oshun's grandmother, smart as she was, was going to be much help.

"Like I said before, Miss Waters, I think the guy's a lunatic. I just hope he's gone by the time I get back to the house."

when I got back from visiting Miss Waters, I found
Brother Mustard Seed sitting at our kitchen table
fooling with a window fan that had quit working. He
had the back of it off and was poking around with a
screwdriver. Daddy's tools were spread out on the
table in front of him, and Mama was standing at the
stove over a skillet of fried chicken.

"Amelia Forrest," he said when I walked in the
back door. Why he called me by both my first and last
name I did not know. I didn't hear him calling Mama
Helen Forrest. Maybe it was a part of what Mama had
said about him being "a little out of the ordinary."

He jumped up out of the chair he was sitting in,
which I might add was mine to begin with, and motioned for me to sit down in it. Mama put the lid on
the skillet and turned around to face me. I just
couldn't get over that red hair of hers. Where in the

world had she gotten the idea that she would look good with red hair? Not from me, I could tell you that much. She hadn't said a word to me about wanting to be a redhead. Her eyebrows weren't red. She didn't have a redhead's features. I didn't get it. I figured I might as well chalk it up to one more thing about the day that I didn't understand. In light of everything else that had happened, my mama getting her natural brown hair dyed red was probably not a very important one, but it bothered me just the same. And on top of everything else, it looked like I would have to deal with this kook through dinner. I took a quick look around the kitchen for his suitcase. It was nowhere in sight. Not a good sign.

"Your mama," Brother Mustard Seed began, "out of the kindness of her big heart, has asked me to stay on here a little while, Amelia Forrest. But now if that's not going to suit you, I'll hit the road right now."

While he was saying this, I tried to read his eyes. I saw a crime fighter's television show one time and an FBI agent told how he looked for little changes in a suspect's eyes. He said a guilty party had a hard time keeping eye contact with you. I would say that Brother Mustard Seed's eye contact was okay, but he did have a little twitch in the corner of his right eye. Not like a major twitch you'd notice if you saw him walking down the street, but it was there.

Since I was busy studying his eyes, I hadn't said anything back to him yet. He took that as a sign to go on. "I'll do my part around here to help out, to fix things that need fixing, to mow the yard, anything. Call me your handyman."

"We don't really have anything that needs fixing," I said. "Except that fan there, and it looks like you're working on it. I guess that'll be all we need. But thank you, anyway. You're welcome to stay for dinner."

"Amelia," Mama said, "I don't think it would hurt anything for Brother Mustard Seed to stay for a while. There's a little painting to be done, some gardening, this and that."

"I'm allergic to paint, ma'am," Brother Mustard Seed said.

Figures, I thought. If you asked me, I'd have said he was allergic to work. After all, he stole a car because he didn't want to work for it.

"What do you say, Amelia? We could use a little help around here."

"And let's not forget that your daddy told me to come here, Amelia Forrest. Sure as I'm standing here in your kitchen, the man stood right in front of me and said to come here and help out, and that's just what I'm doing."

And then, as if to prove his point, he picked up the screwdriver and jabbed it into the motor of the fan.

"You think Daddy meant for you to come here and fix that old broken fan for us?" I asked.

I guess Mama sensed that I was being a smart aleck with my question, so she headed it off. "It's just for a little while, Amelia. He's got a brother who's going to come get him in a few weeks. In the meantime, we'll let him stay here." And then Mama turned around to her skillet and flipped the chicken over.

Well, that's that, I thought to myself. *If they don't want to know what I think, then why do they even ask me?*

Brother Mustard Seed looked at me with a feeble little smile on his face. Mama still had her back to us, so I wrinkled up my nose at him in what I guess you'd call a snarl. If he said anything I was going to say that I had allergies, too, that I had a severe allergy to NUTS! But he didn't say a word, just put his head down and went back to poking at the fan motor.

If he was so good at having visions and all that, maybe he could read minds, too. I glared at him all during dinner and sent my thoughts his way. *I've got your number, buddy. One false move and you're in BIG trouble.*

And, oh, Mama was so chit-chatty. "Here, have some more chicken, Brother Mustard Seed. Like a few more potatoes?" What was causing her to act so silly? Was it those new red curls of hers that sprang up and out all over her head like little springs? Or was it our new handyman sitting there in Daddy's place with corn bread crumbs in his mustache?

During the next few weeks, Brother Mustard Seed finally got the fan to working. Then Mama had him hauling dirt around from place to place in the yard as she set out flowers. He seemed to prefer indoor chores to outdoor chores, though. He liked to plan meals and cook dinners and was always sending Mama to the store for some ingredient that she didn't have. That seemed to be a fine arrangement with Mama as she wasn't all that wild about cooking, anyway.

I mostly stayed out of their way. I read or watched television. I wrote letters to Oshun, and I wrote in my memory book.

One day Mama had Brother Mustard Seed start on Daddy's workshop, sort through the tools and all. He couldn't work at that for long because he got too emotional being around Daddy's stuff. At dinner he would recall conversations he'd had with Daddy in prison and the tears would start coming and he would

have to excuse himself from the table. He was working on Mama's emotions, too. One night, as they
both sat there crying over a plate of spaghetti and
meat sauce, I said, "I've had enough of this." I walked
away from the table and went to my room.

Mama followed me from the kitchen and came in
without even knocking first, which was, generally, a
big no-no in our family. "Amelia, I'm surprised at
you. Was that any way to treat a guest?"

I just looked at her because I really didn't know
what to say. I thought back to what I'd said at the
table, "I've had enough of this." It wasn't so bad,
was it? I mean, it was the truth. I was sick and tired
of all the crying and carrying on at the table
every time Mama and Brother Mustard Seed got
together.

"In a way, it feels good, Amelia, you know? We
hadn't talked about your daddy in a while. I think it
would be good for you if you could just — "

"We hadn't talked about *anything* in a while,
Mama," I interrupted. "Did you ever think about

that? Why is it so easy and so *good for you* to talk to that . . . that . . . that freeloader?"

"Come on, Amelia, the man's not a freeloader. Besides, he's not going to be here that much longer. We'd fallen into a rut, you know? An unhealthy rut. I think Brother Mustard Seed's being here is sort of shaking us out of that. I wish you could see it — could let him help you, too."

"Well, you can forget that right now, because it's not going to happen. Besides, Mama, *I* was going to help us. Who talked you into going to the beauty shop? And I'll say right now for the record that it's not my fault you let them talk you into coloring your hair that strange color. Do you know it's the color of a Halloween pumpkin? I suggested a nice perm, that's all. I guess I should have gone with you."

"Amelia Forrest, listen to yourself! I am a grown woman and I'll do what I like with my hair. I needed a change."

"So, letting that crybaby stay here is another

change, I guess? You're not really falling for that vision stuff, are you, Mama? He's taking us for a ride. Don't you see it? We'll wake up some morning and the TV set will be gone, or worse, he'll murder us in our sleep. Is that the kind of *change* you want?"

"Amelia, don't you think you're being a little dramatic? Let's just drop this for now. I don't think either of us is ready to continue in a civilized manner."

Mama started to leave the room, but then she stopped, turned around, and looked at me for what seemed like a long minute. I thought I heard scurrying outside my bedroom door. I bet anything that the rat had been listening to us.

But if Mama had heard the noise she didn't let on. She said, "I love you, Amelia." And then she stood there and waited. In our family we have a tradition that when somebody says, "I love you," no matter how upset you might be, you are supposed to say, "Back at you." I know it sounds silly, but it's just what we do. I looked at Mama standing there waiting, just waiting for those three words. She still had red eyes from her earlier dinner table boo-hoo fest.

"Back at you, Mama," I finally said to her.

She gave me a wink and said, "Everything's going to be okay."

Funny, that's what Weather Bill always said after a storm. "Everything's going to be okay." Yet there was always another storm and another storm, and even though there might be a stretch of pretty weather in between — you could always count on another storm.

the next afternoon, for Mama's sake, I made a big effort to be friendly. It was raining, so we all settled in with popcorn to watch a silly movie. I didn't even say a word about the fact that Brother Mustard Seed was sitting in the chair where Daddy always sat and was dropping popcorn in between the cushions. On the outside I laughed along with them. But inside I thought to myself, *We are NOT one big happy family. He's leaving soon, and then me and Mama will get back to normal.*

Thinking about him leaving made me feel better, so I decided to stay in and watch the evening news with them, too. The first report was about an explosion over at the feed store in Rapids. The blast demolished the feed store and shook up all the other businesses close by. The newswoman, who happened to have lipstick on her teeth at the time, interviewed the owner of the concrete lawn ornament store next door. The guy was whining about all his concrete animals and his statues of little Dutch boys and girls and how they were all damaged due to the explosion. He stood next to a concrete reindeer that once had a full set of antlers but now had nothing but little stubs sticking out of its head.

Brother Mustard Seed started crying — first, little sniffles, then hard, serious crying. Petey, who had been sitting at Brother Mustard Seed's feet, got up and came over to sit near me. Even Mama looked at him funny this time and didn't rub circles on his back. "Are you okay?" she asked. But he couldn't even answer, just sort of waved his hand her way and kept watching the report. He cried until the news story was over and they went to a commercial break. Then he collected himself, stood up, and looked at us. Instead of being all red-faced from crying, he was pale as a ghost as he left the room. Petey got up to follow him but only made it as far as the basement door before he turned around and came back to me.

"What do you think *that* was all about?" I asked.

"I don't know, Amelia. I don't know about any of

this, but we've told the man he could stay, so let's ride it out," Mama said.

Brother Mustard Seed went down to the basement and didn't even come up for supper, which was pork chops that he'd had marinating since early morning. Mama put the pork chops in the oven, and I figured that when he heard the oven door rattle he'd come on up, but he didn't. When Mama called down to him that supper was ready, he just yelled back, "Go on without me." That was strange. The way he loved to eat, I figured he could gnaw a pork chop down to the bone in nothing flat.

That night when I was in bed I started wondering about what Mama meant when she said, "So let's ride it out." That sounded to me like she might believe in the vision the guy had, at least a little bit. It sounded like she might believe that Daddy had somehow *sent* Brother Mustard Seed to us.

It was funny how in the middle of the day you could sort the things that made sense from the nonsense, but at night it could be harder to do. You started to entertain ideas that you'd never spend two seconds thinking about in the daylight. It was like the night closed in on you and all your good sense got pushed down, too far down to be any help at all.

I started thinking about the vision. If Daddy was going to appear to somebody, why would he come back to somebody like Brother Mustard Seed? Why not to the two people who loved him most in the world? Why not Mama? Why not me?

I wondered if people who died could hold grudges. What if Daddy hated me now? Hated me for what I did. Hated me for playing that stupid joke that took him out of our lives forever? But it was hard to imagine any hate at all in Daddy. I could imagine him being disappointed in me, though.

I pulled out my memory book and turned to a fresh page. I started writing, *Please, please, please, please* — all the way down to the last line of the page, and then I wrote, *Say you still love me.*

I fell asleep and I guess my notebook fell to the floor in the night. When I woke up the next morning it was still turned to that page. In the daylight I was able to sort out my feelings. I knew that Daddy didn't hate me, and he wasn't disappointed in me, or anything. Daddy was gone, and that was that.

I guess I'd like to believe that there was a heaven somewhere and that Daddy was living there and he was happy. But I knew how much he had loved us and our life together here, so if he was there and we weren't, then I knew he couldn't really be happy. And yet, people were supposed to be as happy as all get-out when they were in heaven. It just made no sense. On the other hand, maybe there was a heaven, but when you got there you lost all memory of who you were and of people you knew when you were living. But then, who would you be? You wouldn't really be yourself, would you? More and more it made sense to think that you just lived while you were living and that was it. It was a hard fact, but there it was.

I was sitting at the breakfast table when Brother Mustard Seed came in and broke the news. He'd had a second vision, and he practically tore the basement door off the hinges to come tell us. "Mrs. Forrest, a white holy light descended into your basement last night."

I saw Mama sort of stop in her tracks for just a second, in between the stove and the table, where she was headed with a skillet full of scrambled eggs.

"First things first, Brother Mustard Seed," she said. She motioned for him to take his seat and then she started putting eggs on his plate. Finally, she sat down at the table with the skillet still in her hand. I watched the way the morning sun hit the hairs on top of Mama's head, making it look like those red curls of hers were on fire.

"Was it Jed?" she asked.

"Yes, ma'am, it was. I was sitting there on the sofa

bed, thinking about those busted-up lawn ornaments, feeling just as sad as a man could feel, and not even knowing why. Then the next thing I know, a bright light appeared before me. It felt like somebody was shining a flashlight in my eyes. After some blinking, my eyes adjusted and there he was."

"What did he say?" Mama had such a fierce grip on the wooden skillet handle that her knuckles had turned bone white.

"Well, now, this is kind of the strange part," Brother Mustard Seed said.

I rolled my eyes at this, but nobody saw me because Mama had her eyes on Brother Mustard Seed and he had his eyes closed tight. I thought he might be trying to work up a good cry.

When he opened his eyes, he looked at Mama, and then he reached over, took the skillet out of her hand, and set it down on the table. "Ma'am, your husband said, 'Go get them.'"

Mama sat there letting it sink in. She didn't say anything. Nobody was saying anything.

I decided I would jump in the conversation. They had been treating me like I wasn't even there, and I figured this concerned me as much as it did anybody else. "Get what?" I asked. "The concrete lawn ornaments?"

Brother Mustard Seed looked at me for the first time since he'd come barreling up from the basement. He closed his eyes again like he was concentrating. He put his elbows up on the table and held his head in his hands the way he had on the front porch the first day. When he looked back at me, his eyes were shiny and he looked kind of scared.

"Your daddy didn't say what, but I figured he meant you and your mama," said Brother Mustard Seed.

"Me and Mama? Are you out of your mind?" I said. For some reason, that set Mama off.

"Amelia Forrest! That's enough, okay? I've had enough of your fresh-mouth!" It was not like Mama to yell. She had never been like a lot of the mothers you see on television shows — sassy and loud. Not to say that Mama didn't get mad from time to time, but

she never yelled. She would talk to you about whatever it was and stay calm and even if you wanted to
get mad and raise your voice, you'd feel silly doing it
because she was so calm.

I didn't say a word. Brother Mustard Seed was
looking down at his plate like he was afraid to meet
my eyes or Mama's. There was a strange quiet in the
room — the kind of silence that Miss Waters said happened when an angel held her breath. Nothing
moved or made a noise in those few moments right
after Mama's outburst. Not even Petey. Then she
stood up so fast that her chair turned over behind her.
She picked up the skillet and the spoon and walked
over to the sink and dropped them in with a noisy
clatter like she was trying to break the heavy quiet
that had fallen into her kitchen.

She looked out the window toward Daddy's grass
landing strip. She didn't turn around when Brother
Mustard Seed started talking again.

"Ma'am, I'm as sorry as can be about the tension I
seem to be causing here. Maybe I should be on my

way. I don't want you and your fine daughter to argue. It's just not right. It's not why I'm here."

Finally, Mama turned around to us. She took a deep breath and looked at me. "Amelia, I'm sorry. I think we're all a little on edge about this. But, still, that doesn't excuse me for yelling at you, and it doesn't excuse you for your behavior. You owe Brother Mustard Seed an apology. He's a guest in our house and an adult, and you owe him that respect."

Knowing that there'd be no end to this if I didn't apologize, I muttered a quick, "I'm sorry," in Brother Mustard Seed's direction. He muttered back an "It's okay." I felt like we were both about five years old. I hoped that would be the end of it, but I guess Mama wasn't through with me.

"Now, Amelia, we have a situation here, and none of us really knows what to make of it. I am going to ask for a little more open-mindedness on your part until we can figure out what's going on. Can you give me that much? Can you be open to the fact that there may be more at work here than what meets the eye?"

I didn't answer — I just sat there and looked at the floor.

Getting no response from me, you might expect, would be enough to make Mama yell at me again, but she didn't. She fell right back into her calm mode. "Well, fine, Amelia, I'm not sure what no answer means, but for my part I happen to be curious about this vision. I'm going to exercise my right to be open-minded and ask Brother Mustard Seed to tell us more. If you don't want to hear, you are certainly free to leave the room."

I didn't move. I didn't say anything, but I wasn't about to leave the room. Sure, they'd like that, wouldn't they? I'd leave the house and then come back in an hour, and Mama would meet me at the door with my suitcase and say, "Oh, by the way, Amelia, we're going to run off and live in Timbuktu with this ex-jailbird. I think a little *change* would do us good. Besides, it's what your daddy wants us to do. He sent this man for us!" *Hah! Fat chance! I'm not going anywhere*, I was thinking to myself.

"Go on, Brother Mustard Seed," Mama said, "what else happened?"

"I wish I could tell you more, ma'am, but that's where it ends. Your husband said, 'Go get them.' Then, *poof*, he disappeared. I started blinking my eyes, hoping that I could make the vision return. I prayed and prayed for him to come back. All night long I prayed and blinked."

Mama looked like she was studying on this. She got that little wrinkle in between her eyebrows, and a sort of faraway look in her eyes. Then she turned her attention to me. "Amelia, it's your turn now if you want to take it. What do you make of all this? I know you have an opinion. I think it's time we put it all out on the table."

What was I supposed to say? Or maybe a better question was, what did she want to hear? If I said what I really thought, would she yell at me again? I kept thinking, *Well, he'll be gone soon, so I'll try to keep my mouth shut.* I guess I wanted to think that Mama still had her good senses and knew that there wasn't anything to this vision business, but I wasn't sure. What was all this talk about "more at work here than meets the eye"? About being "open-minded"? Was she still just helping him get back on his feet, or had she started believing in the visions? I had hoped that the brother Mama mentioned would finally show up and collect this misfit before things got out of hand. But it seemed like things were getting out of hand right before my very eyes.

Is this what happens when you stop going to church? Because, for the most part, we had. We went for a little while after Daddy died, and then our attendance sort of tapered off. It seemed like the kind of thing that was always more important to Daddy than to Mama, anyway. Not that Mama didn't do just as much to help out people as he did. I guess she just did it in a way that seemed like a regular part of everyday living. She was always taking food to people, sitting with the sick, and so on. Daddy was the one who had gotten most of the church mission programs started. I guess what I'm saying is that I wasn't quite sure how Mama felt about God, religion, miracles, or any of that stuff. And I sure as heck couldn't say for certain how she felt about visions. Maybe she was thinking that the vision was Daddy's way to get us to go back to church or something. Maybe she thought Daddy was trying to tell her how disappointed he was that she wasn't carrying on all the programs he had started.

Actually, I couldn't tell you what she was thinking. All I knew was that this troublemaker claimed to have had a second vision, and he seemed to think it involved taking me and Mama off somewhere. Mama was now asking me what I thought, and even said, "Lay it out on the table," so lay it out, I did. What did I have to lose?

"I don't believe in your crackpot visions. I didn't believe in the first one and I don't believe in this one, especially since it doesn't make a whole lot of sense. Besides, I've got news for you, Buster, you're not taking us anywhere. If you want to know the truth, I don't believe in much of anything anymore except for accidents."

Brother Mustard Seed reached across the table and put his chubby red hand over mine. "You don't believe in much of anything?" he said. He looked from me to Mama and then back at me again.

I guess I expected Mama to let me have it. I had violated all the rules about respect for the houseguest and the adult and all that business. Plus, I'd just said that I didn't believe in anything. I had never said anything like that before.

Mama was looking out across the long, grassy strip where she used to watch Daddy's plane come gliding in like a big white bird. When she turned around I saw that she was wearing that fake smile that she put on whenever people from the church came by to tell us that they missed having us there.

"Amelia believes in God," Mama said to Brother Mustard Seed, but she was looking at me as she said it. "She was baptized in the Corinth River and is a member of the Corinth Baptist Church. That was two years ago, wasn't it, Amelia? It's just that these visions, Brother Mustard Seed . . . well, I think it takes a more mature spirit to be able to accept them. I, for one, believe that if Jed Forrest is trying to send us word through you, then he's got a good reason for it and we'd better be open and ready to receive the message. I'm sure this will all make sense in time."

"Hallelujah, Mrs. Forrest! Believe me when I say I don't mean to cause any pain or suffering. I don't know why I'm here myself. All I know is that I'm trying to follow the instructions from your precious husband, bless his soul."

Mama picked up her chair off the floor, sat back down at the table, then reached over and put a biscuit on Brother Mustard Seed's plate. "Well, that's good enough for me. We'll just see what happens next, won't we?" she said. And then she looked at me, "Won't we, Amelia?"

"Well, you're right about one thing, Mama," I

said. "I was baptized in the Corinth River. But that river's nothing but an old swimming hole full of beer cans and pieces of Styrofoam coolers. It's where the teenagers go to get drunk and fool around. The whole time I was in the water I was scared that a water moccasin would bite me on the leg. After I got dunked I came sputtering up out of that nasty old river and didn't feel a bit holier than when I went in. Two days later, if you'll remember, I caught a chest cold."

After my little speech I stood up from the table, grabbed a biscuit, and walked out the back door. I went straight to the middle of the runway, sat down, and thought about the things I had just said.

Accidents! Who did I think I was kidding? Had I really said that I didn't believe in anything but accidents? Like I believed Daddy's crash was just some freaky accident that didn't have a thing to do with me? I caused it. I did it. And nothing was ever going to change that, and Daddy was never going to come back. Not in real life, and not because some fat old ex-convict dreamed him up.

Why did everything have to get so complicated? I looked up at blue sky and remembered what it felt like to be up there — above everything. Sometimes Daddy would let me fly his plane. I would hold the stick and look down at the little farms and towns that I was flying over and I felt like I never wanted to come down. The whole world looked better from up there. Neat and squared off, not messy like it really was.

I remembered one of the first times I had flown with Daddy. We took off and flew for miles and miles. I could see everything. "Look at the cars, Daddy! I see a train on a railroad track! There's a town! I see a shopping mall! The cars all lined up in straight rows! Is that the river where we swim? It's crooked like a snake."

At last he said, "We'd better head back now, Amelia." But I wasn't ready to head back. It seemed like no matter how far we flew, there was always something else up ahead that I wanted to see. Finally, he said, "I'm going to go back now before we go too far and fall off the edge of the world. But we'll have a contest to make it more interesting. The first person to see home wins."

This is what I wrote in my memory book about that day:

I can see our house, Daddy! It looks so little, like a toy!

Do you see your mama, Amelia? She's right there, in the front yard. Look, Amelia, she's waving at us.

I see her!

You want to make the plane wave back? Here we go!

Mama's waving, Daddy! She's jumping up and down and laughing!

I couldn't eat the biscuit because there was a lump in my throat that the biscuit couldn't get past. I crumbled it up and threw it out for the birds to find. The birds still landed on Daddy's strip — probably more birds than ever because it had all gone to seed. I wished that Mama would have it mowed. I was sitting down, and the weeds came up over my head.

That first day that Brother Mustard Seed showed up it felt like the day was swallowing me up whole. Now, sitting here in the middle of the weeds, I felt like I had finally landed in the belly of the beast. I thrashed my arms around and whacked at the springy weeds like a crazy person. "Take that! And that! And that!" I shouted and punched at them. They just popped right back up in my face.

My legs had started to itch from sitting in the weeds so long. Before I knew it, I had scratched big welts on both legs. Daddy would never have let his landing strip get all grown up with weeds. Never. And he told me to keep the runway clear. To take care of things. I probably deserved all the scratching I was having to do.

I guess I kind of hoped that Mama would come out to see about me, but she was probably too busy listening to the nutty, ex-convict car thief carry on. I decided to visit Miss Waters again — maybe she would be more helpful in the answer department this time.

When I got there she was standing over a big open box that she had just received from Oshun's parents in Haiti.

"Well, just in time!" Miss Waters said. "There's something for you in here."

She handed me a small package wrapped in brown paper and a letter written on the side of a grocery sack instead of on regular stationery. Who knew why Oshun did the crazy things that she did?

Her letter was long. She said they were learning some weird things about different religions and cultures. Then she went on and on, kind of bragging, I thought, about how she found out that she's named Oshun after an African goddess — the goddess of sweet water and love. She said that she would bring back some river stones that had been blessed in a fountain built to worship the Oshun goddess.

When I read the letter to Miss Waters, she said, "Ooh, that girl's gonna be hard to live with when she gets back to the real world. Sounds like she's got the big head from all this Oshun goddess nonsense."

I said I thought so, too. After all, I was named after Amelia Earhart, the great woman pilot, but you didn't see me going around bragging about it.

Then I read the last part of Oshun's letter.

Remember, Amelia, we said that I should find a voodoo doll that looked like ol' P. E. Pascal, and

that we would stick pins in it if he tried to make us
run laps? Well, I found a doll. I don't think it
looks much like Pascal, but I decided to buy it,
anyway. I'll keep looking for a Pascal doll.
Luv ya, miss ya,
OSHUN
Goddess of Sweet Water and LOVE

I unwrapped the brown package and took out the doll. Oshun was right: It looked nothing like Mr. Pascal, who is a tall, skinny, black-haired man with a whistle between his lips all the time.

The doll was made of white cloth, and the face was stitched on with little black threads. There was grayish hair stuck to the top of its head, and it had a scraggly mustache made of the same gray hair. The hair was coarse, like the hair of a horse's tail. The doll was pudgy around its middle — stuffed tight with cotton, I guess. And then I noticed a tiny blue stitch under its left eye. I looked closer. It was shaped like a tear.

The gray hair sticking up kind of wild-like, the mustache covering his top lip, the fat stomach, the tear! It hit me like a ton of bricks: Oshun had sent me a doll that looked *exactly* like Brother Mustard Seed.

Miss Waters looked over my shoulder at the doll. I gave it to her. It felt warm in my hands — I didn't like holding it.

"Well, now, isn't this something." She turned the doll over and looked at it from all sides. Then she gave it back to me. "That's some gift, Amelia. Looks just like something Oshun would pick out. Don't you think?"

"Miss Waters, you're going to think I'm crazy, but it looks like that ex-convict I told you about — the one who's living with us."

"Is that right? It looks like him? Well, now, I haven't met your houseguest, but if he looks like this doll, I'd say he's pleasant enough, just a little on the sad side."

"I wouldn't call it the sad side, Miss Waters, more

like the *insane* side. And it seems to me that Mama's following right along behind him."

She laughed, but I didn't know why, because it wasn't funny.

"Amelia," she said, "your daddy said to me once, 'That girl of mine has her head in the clouds just like me, but her feet never leave the ground.'"

"Daddy said that? What's that supposed to mean?"

"I'm not sure, Amelia. I guess there's a couple of different ways of looking at it," she said. "But I do know that sometimes you've just got to let your feet leave the ground."

Then she did a funny thing. She touched the blue tear on the doll and then she touched my cheek, right under my left eye. But I had no tear. I hadn't had tears in a long, long time.

I told her I needed to get on back home. I needed some time to think about the strange things that were happening. I needed to remind myself that it was all a bunch of coincidences. It's just that when a lot of coincidences started happening at the same time, you couldn't help but feel a little strange. It made you start to wonder about everything, and I didn't like to wonder about everything. I liked to know what was what.

When I got back to the house and walked into the kitchen I didn't see Brother Mustard Seed anywhere around. I figured maybe he was off somewhere having himself another one of his flashlight-in-the-eyes visions. My mama was on the phone, and I heard her say, "Well, whenever you can get around to it, Jerry Ray, but the sooner the better."

I stood there in the kitchen until she got off the phone. I had the doll and Oshun's letter all wrapped up in the package. I hadn't decided yet if I wanted to show Mama. But I had decided that I wanted some answers. I deserved to know what was going on. Oshun had always said, "Get to the bottom of things." That seemed to be good advice in this case.

I stood there just scratching my legs and thinking

about everything I wanted to know, while Mama was on the phone. Number one, I wanted to know the exact date that Brother Mustard Seed would be leaving with his brother. Number two, I wanted to know exactly what Mama thought about the visions. Either she believed in them or not. Simple as that. And if it turned out that she *did* believe in the visions, then, number three, I wanted to know if Mama was entertaining *any* idea whatsoever about going somewhere with Brother Mustard Seed, since he'd been spouting off with that "Go get them" vision. I had a lot on my mind and hoped we could get things cleared up with one good housecleaning conversation.

Mama hung up the phone with a cheery "Bye-bye, now!" And then she said to me, "Jerry Ray's going to come out tomorrow morning and mow the field. It's a real mess out there."

"Is that what it is now, Mama? Just a field?" I asked her. "It used to be a landing strip, remember? A big, long, grass runway where Daddy used to land his crop-dusting plane."

"Amelia, what's wrong with you? I didn't mean anything by calling it a field. But, after all, it *is* a field."

"No! Say it, Mama. Say it's a runway."

"Stop it, Amelia! Of course, it's your daddy's runway. I thought you'd be happy that we're getting it mowed. I saw you sitting out there after your little speech this morning. The weeds were over your head."

"Yeah, well, I think the question is, why are we just now getting it mowed? Did Brother Mustard Seed have a vision and tell you Daddy said, 'Mow it'? It seems like nothing really gets done around here until that little creep makes some announcement."

"Look, Amelia, you're going too far. If you want to talk about this, we'll talk, but if you're just trying to get me to send Brother Mustard Seed away because you don't like the way he looks, or the way he acts, or that he's a little peculiar, or that he messed up some summer plans you had, I won't do it — not yet. When I said that before about there being more to this than meets the eye, I meant it. I can't say how I know it, but it just seems like there's some unfinished business . . . your daddy was taken from us too suddenly. I guess what I'm saying is that I don't know what's on the other side. I don't even know for sure that there *is* another side, but if there is one, and your daddy's there, I know he'd do everything in his power to make things better for us."

"But, Mama, would he send some ex-convict to live with us? Is that what he'd do?"

"He would if that was the only way to get our attention," Mama said. "Would you like it better if he sent a letter? A telegram? Appeared in a television commercial?"

"Do you really believe it, Mama, I mean believe with all your heart that Daddy's come back in some kind of hocus-pocus light show? That the only one who can see him is that gray-haired little troll living in our basement? And that now Daddy's told him he should come here and 'get us,' whatever that means. Is that what you believe, or do you just *want* to believe it?"

"I'm not sure there's much difference, Amelia. You believe because you want to. I think I want to, right now, how about you?"

For a minute I wanted to say yeah, that I'd like to believe, too, that maybe, just maybe, I could find out if Daddy still loved me and didn't blame me for what I'd done. I guess that was my unfinished business. But I couldn't bring myself to say it. There were way too many risks.

I was standing in front of Mama, and when she put her hands up on my shoulders I realized for the first time that we were the same height. For some reason that made me feel stronger than Mama. I straightened up my posture, making me a fraction taller.

"Oh, Amelia, you don't have to be so hard. I know your daddy bragged that you were one tough cookie, and you are. But you don't have to be, not all the time. Can't you at least believe in the *possibility* that your daddy's trying to contact us, maybe even help us, through this man?"

I saw that my mama wanted, more than anything,

for me to believe that Daddy was reaching out to us. But I couldn't do it. If I did, then I'd have to accept anything that Brother Mustard Seed told us, and I refused to do that.

"No," I said. "If Daddy wants to reach out to somebody, then let him reach out to you or to me. But not this Brother Mustard Seed. I'm afraid, Mama. He could tell you *anything* right now and if he told you that Daddy said it in a vision, then you'd go along with it."

"Oh, that's not true, Amelia. I know that there may be nothing to this after all."

"Let me ask you something, Mama, and answer me honestly. If Brother Mustard Seed came to you right now and said that he had a vision and Daddy told him we should sell this place and move off somewhere else, would you believe him? Would you do it?"

"Amelia, for your information, I have thought that it might be good for us to sell this house and move into town. We don't need a place this big and so far out in the country — and with that runway out there reminding me every time I see it that Jed's not coming back . . . yeah, I've thought about it, and I bet your daddy would think it's a good idea, too."

I couldn't believe what I was hearing. "Mama, that's what I've been trying to tell you. You're letting that Brother Mustard Seed put ideas in your head. It's a good thing I didn't go on vacation with Oshun. You probably would have sold everything right out from under me. We were going along just fine until that kook showed up and started filling your new, curly red head with nonsense!"

Mama turned away from me. She looked up at the fireplace mantel, and for the first time I noticed that Daddy's picture wasn't there. Then she turned again and looked me straight in the eye.

"Let me tell you something, young lady, I'll believe what I want to believe for as long as I want to believe it, and right now I want to believe in the visions and try to figure out what they mean for us. And another thing — you say we were going along just fine? You, a straight-A student, almost failed sixth grade, and I put on fifty pounds all because I couldn't do anything else but try to fill up some empty place inside with junk food. And, even though it's none of your business, my hair will continue to be red until I decide to change it to something else!"

I knew I should have stopped then, but I didn't. "Mama, if you think for a minute that I'm going to sit around and let that stupid phony talk you into selling our home and taking us to God-knows-where, then I guess you're just as nutty as he is. I'll run away before I'll go anywhere with that phony baloney." As I was talking I was sort of shaking the package that Oshun had sent and using it as a pointer. Just as I said "phony baloney," the Brother Mustard Seed doll went flying across the room and landed on the fireplace hearth.

At the *same* time, we heard a racket in the basement that reminded me of the noise made when I accidentally knocked over a pyramid display of canned cling peaches at the Houchens store — one big crash followed by a series of smaller crashes. But unlike the cling peaches incident, this crash was followed by a loud moan.

when we got to the basement, we found Brother Mustard Seed sitting on the floor, holding his foot. The stepladder he'd been using was turned over sideways on the floor and Petey had taken cover in the corner. While Mama was tending to his foot and asking him about what happened, I got a good look at what he'd been up to.

High up on the wall, directly in front of the sofa bed, Brother Mustard Seed had hung Daddy's picture — the one from our fireplace mantel.

Then, around the picture, in a big swirl starting at the center, where Daddy's picture was, he had strung Christmas lights — in the middle of summer — as far out as he could go with them, *and* he already had them plugged in.

"I think I stapled into one of the electric wires. I felt a jolt — a big jolt — *whoosh!* It went through me and knocked me clean off the ladder! Lord, my heart's racing!"

Mama peeled the sock off the foot he was holding. I had a lot of questions for the guy that were just begging to be answered, like who told him he could take my daddy's picture off the fireplace mantel? And where did he get the bright idea to put up Christmas lights — probably *our* Christmas lights — in July? And didn't he think it was kind of stupid to staple up electric lights while you had them plugged in? And, last but not least, hadn't anybody ever told him that you don't climb an aluminum stepladder in your sock feet, since anybody with half a brain would know that aluminum steps are slick? But, like I said, it was apparent the guy was in pain, and I didn't think my questions would have been welcome.

I could see that his foot was swelling up and turning blue.

"We're going to have to get you to the emergency

room. I think this foot might be broken," Mama said. "Come on, Amelia, let's help him up."

"I believe I can get up on my own power, ma'am," he said. After watching him struggle for a while, we finally had to step in and help him get to his feet, which wasn't easy.

"You think you can hop on your good foot up the basement stairs?" Mama asked him. "You can hold on to the rail, and we'll help."

After a lot of hopping, stopping, and moaning, Brother Mustard Seed finally made it up to the kitchen. We got him out the door and into the front seat of the car.

"I'm going to stay here, Mama."

She gave me a strange look. I knew that she was remembering what I'd said about running away. "Why don't you ride with us to the hospital, Amelia?"

"No, Mama," I said. "I've got stuff here I want to do."

"We'll figure all this out, Amelia, I promise.

Okay? I'm not going to sell the house out from under you. It's a decision we'll make together."

"Yeah, maybe," I said, and then I turned away from her and the big human accident she had in the car with her.

When I got inside, I remembered that I'd left my M encyclopedia in the living room. I think the last time I'd done any studying was the day that Brother Mustard Seed showed up and got this hornet's nest stirred up for us.

The first thing I saw when I walked in there was that little doll on the floor where it had landed when I sent it sailing across the room. But that had just been an accident — it had slipped out of my hands, that's all. It was just a coincidence that the man fell off the ladder at the same time.

I didn't have anything to do with it! Brother Mustard Seed was the one dumb enough to be up on a ladder in his socks. He was the one dumb enough to be stapling into live electric wires.

The doll had landed faceup. Its beady little eyes

seemed to be looking at me. I picked it up, and just like before, it felt warm in my hands. I wanted to throw it in the garbage can — but the first thing that popped in my head was that Brother Mustard Seed was in the car with my mama.

I just stood there in the living room, holding the stupid doll, looking for something familiar, anything to make me feel like I wasn't going crazy.

I wanted my daddy. I looked up at the fireplace mantel. But, of course, his picture wasn't there. It was hanging on a wall in the basement surrounded by about a hundred twinkling Christmas lights. Petey was yapping his head off at the front door, so I let him in.

I went up to my room and looked around. I put the doll on my bookshelf at the end of the encyclopedias. And then I started thinking, *What if that* XYZ *encyclopedia falls over on the doll?* Then I put it in an empty shoe box that I found in my closet. But I thought, *Hmmm, I'd better punch holes in the top of the box so that air can get in.* It was when I was punching holes in the shoe box with a pen that I thought about

what I was doing — *Whoa! Back up the train, Amelia,
you're acting as crazy as the rest of them!*

Petey had jumped up on the bed with me. He had
his head turned sort of sideways the way he does
sometimes. He looked like he wanted to tell me
something. I wished he could talk. I wished he would
just say, "Amelia, calm down, you're going off the
deep end, girl."

But, of course, Petey didn't say a word. And at that
moment I decided I didn't need a dog to tell me what
I knew already. There was enough crazy-thinking
going on without my adding to it. I put the doll on
my bed with my stuffed animals and went outside.

I had some thinking to do and figured the best
place to do it would be out on the landing strip. It was
kind of nice to hide there in the middle of the weeds
with nothing but the flat blue sky above you. I didn't
even care if my legs started itching again. Maybe
Mama would come back and not find me in the house
and think that I really had run away. That would
show her.

Lying on my back, I stretched my arms and legs out like you do when you make a snow angel. But I didn't move. You couldn't make an angel out of those weeds. I might leave a flat place when I got up, but that's all. Besides, I didn't want to move. I wanted to figure things out, and that was something you had to do from a quiet and still place in your head.

I faced the direction that Daddy usually flew in when the wind was right. You have to know about wind direction and clouds and storms and so many other things when you fly. Daddy used to have a wind sock hanging from a pole at one end of the field, but it was gone now. Not long after the crash, Mama had one of the Ray brothers come take it down and even take the pole out of the ground and haul it away. She said it bothered her to look out her kitchen window and see that wind sock blowing around up there. And now she was thinking about moving us away because she didn't like seeing the runway, either. She said it reminded her of Daddy. Did I remind her of Daddy, too? Did it bother her to look at me?

The sun was in my eyes and I squinted, but through the sun squints I saw something dark against the blue sky. Whatever it was, was heading my way, and was coming in lower and lower. I sat up to get a better look.

It was a flock of birds, big blackbirds, like crows or vultures or something. They weren't flying in any sort of formation like you usually see a big group of birds flying in. These birds were just flying and squawking in a big, disorganized mess.

I first thought of running to the house. I saw a movie once about a bunch of birds that just took over a town and pecked up a lot of people, and I have to say it was one of the scariest movies I had ever seen. But I didn't run to the house. I didn't move.

The birds touched down on the landing strip about the same time and then they just scattered in the weeds. They were making weird noises — almost like a croak — as they pecked at the ground.

They were far enough from me that I didn't feel afraid. But, suddenly, one bird sort of flew up and away from the rest of the group and landed right at the end of my feet. It was the blackest bird I'd ever seen. Even its beak and feet were black. Its chest and the tips of its wings were sort of purply-black and shiny. In a way, it looked like a plain old crow, but it was too big to be a crow. I wondered what it was. I had never seen any bird like it before.

The next thing I knew, the bird opened its beak and pecked at my shoestring. Then he pulled it. I didn't know what to do. I was afraid if I kicked or made a sudden move the bird might attack me, just like in the movie.

Finally, it dropped my shoestring and just stood there and looked at me really hard. Sort of turned its head to the side and back again. It felt like it was trying to get a good look at me, first with one eye and then with the other. I had never had a bird study me that way, and I did not get a good feeling from it.

"Stop it! Go away!" I yelled. The bird flew back to join the rest of its gang. They pecked around among the weeds for a while longer, and then the whole flock just sort of lifted off and flew back the way they'd come in. Just like that and the birds were gone.

I remembered something Daddy had said one time about birds. He'd said, "I get the feeling that birds laugh at me behind my back. Look at 'em — they just fly around and land like it's nothing. But I have to study and practice and study and practice and every time I fly, it still takes my full concentration. They don't have to do a thing! They just fly. I bet they're just laughing their feathered tails off at me for trying so hard to be like them."

I think I knew what he meant. But I wasn't sure if the bird that pecked at my shoestring was laughing at me. I thought he looked confused, or maybe surprised — yeah, that was it: He seemed surprised to find me sitting there in the middle of the weeds.

11

when Mama finally got back with Brother Mustard Seed, I was sitting back in the cool shadows on the front porch reading about birds in the encyclopedia. Before he was even out of the car with his cast and his crutches, I could hear him. It sounded like he was preaching a sermon. I could hear Mama, too. She was calling, "Amelia! Amelia, where are you?"

"A little bone! A tiny little bone on the side of a foot," Brother Mustard Seed was hollering. "No bigger than a chicken bone, and it can bring a man down. It's God's way of saying, 'Don't get too big for your britches, Mustard Seed.'"

After he hauled himself out of the car, he leaned against it and raised one crutch high in the air. He yelled to me, "I've learned my lesson, Amelia Forrest!"

I walked over to the steps and called out, "I'm here." Mama looked relieved when she saw me up on the porch. Maybe she thought I really had run away.

She started helping Brother Mustard Seed hobble up to the porch. I hoped the lesson he said he'd learned was a safety lesson.

He was a disaster with the crutches. He finally made it to the porch and slumped into the chair next to mine. He stuck his broken foot out in front of him. I saw then that his foot was not in a real cast, but in a funny kind of shoe with a hard bottom and cloth sides. His toes were sticking out the end and looked like little pink sausages.

"You didn't get a cast?" I asked him.

"It's a tiny little bone, just a little thing on the side, it's the one connected to my little toe."

Oh boy, I thought, *he's going to start preaching about chicken bones again.* But he didn't. He got back to the question I asked him.

"The doctor said that this little ol' bone will heal up in no time. Put my foot in this soft-shoe cast. It's my first broken bone, Amelia Forrest. Have you ever had one?"

"Nope. I'm a very careful person," I told him.

This would have been a good time to go into the whole safety issue thing, but I didn't figure he would listen, and if he did listen, I didn't think he would remember.

"To tell you the truth, I was sort of hoping for a real cast," he said. "You know how people get a leg or arm broke and then get their friends to write messages on the cast? Well, I was sort of hoping to get a cast so I could get some of them little Get Well messages."

When he said that I was thinking, *That's one of the dumbest things I've ever heard — to wish for a broken bone so people can write things on your cast.* But then, I remembered a couple of years ago when Oshun broke her arm and she got a bright green cast that went all the way from her hand up past her elbow. Everybody at school flocked around her and wrote things and drew pictures on her cast, but she saved the elbow part for me, which was a sweet thing to do. I drew a bull's-eye on the elbow section of her cast with different-colored markers. I have to say, I was a little bit jealous of that cast and all the attention it got her.

"What did you mean when you said you learned your lesson?" I asked him.

Before he could answer, Mama got up and said that she would fix us all some iced tea. I figured she'd been listening to this story all the way home from the hospital and didn't feel the need to hear it again. She touched the top of my head on her way to the door, and sort of let it linger there. When Mama opened the door, Petey came bounding outside and settled down next to Brother Mustard Seed.

"Well, I was trying to bring on a vision, Amelia. I was trying to encourage — or you might say *lure* — your daddy's vision back," he said.

"By putting up his picture in the middle of a bunch of Christmas lights?"

"I thought I'd try meditating on Brother Jed's picture. I figured if it was surrounded by all those twinkling lights, then the vision might reappear. Every time I've had a vision, there's been a light involved in some way. At the prison I saw that ball of light in the tree that turned into a column of light and then — *boom* — there was your daddy! Then last night I got that bright light in my eyes — felt sort of like a deer getting caught in the headlights. Once my eyes stopped watering — *boom* — there was your daddy again! Anyhow, I thought the Christmas lights might help bring him back."

For a moment I had a mean thought about getting up, stomping off the porch, and *accidentally* knocking into that ugly, blue, swollen foot of his. But I decided to be mean with words instead. Just when I was *sort of* starting to think about him as a normal human being who can really break bones and get hurt and all, he had to go and say something stupid like that.

"Nothing's gonna bring my daddy back," I snapped. "Don't you know anything? You pretend to have these silly visions, but all you're doing is putting ideas in Mama's head and making me mad. I don't know exactly what you're up to, but whatever it is, I don't like it. If you had really been Daddy's friend, you'd see what you're doing to us and you'd leave us alone."

He started crying. Then he looked at me with his big old wet face and said, "I was your daddy's friend. I really was. And he liked me, too, even from the start. Sinner that I was, he waltzed right into that prison and accepted me just like that. He helped turn me around. My brother and I grew up in the Baptist Children's Home just outside of Louisville. I don't know what happened to our daddy and mama. My brother knows, but he's older and he never would tell me. All we had was each other. My brother grew up to be a good man, got a family and a good job. When I stole the car he washed his hands of me, said I was turning out to be trash just like our folks. I didn't want to be trash, Amelia. I wanted to be good, but I took a wrong turn."

He stopped talking then and looked at me like he expected me to say something about the life of hard knocks that he'd had. But I'd had hard knocks, too.

"That reminds me of something your daddy said about you one time. You want to hear it?"

"Daddy talked to you about me?" I asked.

"Oh, he talked about you a lot. One time when you were just learning to walk, your daddy said you would toddle off here and there. He said, 'I have to walk along behind her all the time or she'll start to veer off in the wrong direction, maybe head for the steps, and I'll nudge her around. That's all it takes. Just a little nudging.' I felt like that's what he was doing with me, just nudging me back around in a kind and gentle way. That was your daddy, Amelia Forrest."

What else could this man tell me about Daddy? He said my daddy liked him and accepted him right from the start. How was he able to do that? This man was a thief. He took something that didn't belong to him. He broke the law. And he was a little on the weird side, too. But Daddy didn't hold any of that against him, just figured he went in the wrong direction and needed a little nudging back to the right way. Is that what Daddy would think about me? Even though what I did was a lot worse than stealing a car?

I glanced over at Brother Mustard Seed sitting

there with his broken foot sticking out in front of him, sniffling and crying a little bit. Petey licked Brother Mustard Seed's toes and then put his head up in the man's lap, waiting to get it scratched. Almost from the first night, Petey had been sleeping in the basement with him. I guess, in a way, Petey had accepted Brother Mustard Seed from the start, too. No questions asked.

"Brother Mustard Seed," I said. "I want to ask you something, and let me tell you, it's not an easy thing for me to ask."

"Anything, Amelia Forrest, anything at all."

"Did you really, I mean, *really*, see my daddy in a vision? You're not just making it up?"

"No, ma'am, I most certainly am *not* making it up, and may God strike me dead with lightning if I'm lying. I saw your daddy a total of two times now, and both times he spoke to me."

"Okay, then, I've got another question." I was taking the Oshun approach. I was getting to the bottom of things. "Now this second time, when he said,

'Go get them,' do you think he meant for you to get me and Mama? Is that what you really think?"

"I'll tell you now, when he first spoke those words to me, the thing that popped in my head was that I was supposed to get you and your mama, but then I don't know what I was supposed to do with you after that — you know what I mean? It seemed like an incomplete vision, so I figure I'm just waiting on the third one now. I know that you're not happy about this at all, so that's why I was working so hard to bring on another one with the Christmas lights. Maybe he didn't mean you and your mama — maybe he meant go get something else — like the concrete animals, for instance. You mentioned them at the breakfast table, Amelia Forrest, and when you said it, I thought, *Hmmm, maybe that's what I'm supposed to get.* I just don't know."

"Did you know that now Mama's talking about selling this place? Do you think you put that idea in her head?"

"No-sir-ee, I did not. That first day I came here,

your mama was telling me how hard it had been on the both of you this last year. She said she wondered if it might not be easier to just start out somewhere else, somewhere new. Memories can be hard to live with, Amelia Forrest."

I thought about that. Why hadn't Mama talked to me about how she was feeling? But, then again, this past year I hadn't done much talking to Mama, either. And I had plenty I should have told her.

When Mama came back out on the porch, she took a look at Brother Mustard Seed and then at me. He still looked a little teary-eyed from the cry he'd had when I'd first let him have it. I guess she was wondering what all I might have said to him this time. I just shrugged my shoulders at Mama as if to say, "The crybaby is at it again."

"What's going on?" she asked. "Nobody's fighting? Everybody's being nice? Am I at the right house?" Mama was looking at me when she said it.

"Nice as pie, ma'am. Nice as a lemon custard pie." Brother Mustard Seed pulled his bandanna out of his pocket and dabbed at his face. "Me and Amelia Forrest were just talking about these . . . these beautiful birds here." He reached over and took the encyclopedia out of my lap. "We were just talking about God's great wonders of the sky, and I guess I got a little emotional."

From the look on Mama's face, she wasn't buying the "great wonders of the sky" bit.

Brother Mustard Seed looked down and, for the first time, saw the picture he was pointing to. "What do you know!" he said. "I believe these are the same birds I saw in the oak tree when I had the prison yard vision. Now here they are in this book."

I had just been reading about the birds that he was pointing to. They were ravens — the same ones that had landed on Daddy's runway that morning.

Mama looked over Brother Mustard Seed's shoulder at the picture of the dark birds.

"I saw them, too, Mama. They're ravens," I told her. "A whole gang of them landed out on the runway today. One of them flew down to my foot and pulled on my shoestring."

She put the tray of iced tea down on a little table and took the book from Brother Mustard Seed. He was still pointing to the picture of the birds with his big pink finger.

"That's them, all right," he said. "They squawked and flapped around in that tree, and a few of them flew down to the ground. I got a good look at them — next thing I knew, *whoosh!* They lifted up and flew off like a big, dark cloud."

"We've got plenty of crows around here," Mama said. "But I don't think I've ever seen any of these."

"Read it out loud, Mrs. Forrest. Read about the ravens to us," Brother Mustard Seed said.

He wriggled around in his seat, trying to get at the iced tea. I saw Mama look at me, so I reached over and handed him a glass before he fell out of his chair and required a second trip to the hospital.

Mama began to read:

"'The raven is a member of the crow family. It can be recognized by its large size, measuring about twenty-six inches in length.'"

"We already know what they look like, Mama, they look like big crows," I told her. "Read the next section, called 'The Raven Trickster.'"

I had already read it. I'd read everything in that encyclopedia about the ravens as soon as I found out they were the birds that had landed on my daddy's runway. I wanted to know everything about that purple-black bird that had pecked at my shoestring and studied me with its curious eyes.

"'The raven has been the object of countless myths and legends around the world,'" Mama continued. "'Many Native American peoples considered Raven to be the god who brought life and order, joy and laughter. In one legend, the raven is described as a trickster who tries to steal light from the sun. In his mischievous attempt, he scorches himself and blackens his feathers.'"

Brother Mustard Seed had finished off his tea. He slurped on the ice cubes but he stopped long enough to comment on his sighting of the ravens in the prison yard.

"When I think about it — it was strange. Real, real strange. First I saw the light in the tree, then the light comes down and turns into the vision of Jed Forrest. Then the vision's gone, and there's a big flock of birds up in the tree. They flapped around and squawked, almost like they were laughing. They were having a big old time. Tricksters. Your daddy was a trickster, Amelia! One time he put a plastic banana in a sack of fruit he brought me. Looked just like a real banana!"

Brother Mustard Seed laughed and slapped his knee. When he did, he jarred his broken foot. He went from laughing about the plastic banana to crying out, "Oooh, that hurt like the devil!"

Mama looked at him. "I'm sorry, ma'am, I didn't

mean to say 'devil.' It's prison talk — I reckon when a fellow hears language like that every day, some of it's bound to rub off."

"You can say 'devil.' We don't care," I told him.

"Yes, we do care. We'd prefer not to hear it," said Mama. "Now if you don't mind, I'll finish reading this."

She cleared her throat. It's funny, when she used to read me bedtime stories, she always cleared her throat like that before beginning — sort of a little cough. My first-grade teacher told Mama that whenever she called on me to read in school, I always did the same thing, like I thought that's what you had to do in order to read.

Mama's voice was louder this time, I guess to drown out the slurping noise that Brother Mustard Seed made with the ice cubes — another bad habit I figured he'd picked up in prison.

"'Many myths about the raven have to do with his helpful, nurturing spirit. Even his tricks are seen as ways to teach people to laugh at their own follies. The raven is believed to be one of the most curious and intelligent of all birds. One legend describes the raven as the "Seeker of Secrets." His great curiosity leads him to gather information and to uncover secrets. He believes that his search for the truth is the reason for his being.'"

"Interesting bird. Real interesting bird," Brother Mustard Seed said.

"I always thought that seeing a raven was supposed to bring bad luck," said Mama. "But this makes it seem — well, almost human. Sort of a funny, smart, helping human."

Brother Mustard Seed said, "Just like Jed Forrest." And I said, "Just like Daddy." And our words, spoken at the same time, caused all three of us to jump.

the next morning I had a new dream to write about in my memory book.

> My dream starts out like the old one. Daddy is flying his plane on a moonless night, and I am watching him from below. I hear the pop and I know that he's in trouble.
>
> I yell at him to throw out the canned goods and I see the cans start falling to the earth. I run to keep from getting hit over the head and I find myself in an open field. Then I hear something behind me. The canned goods are chasing me! The cans of tuna, beans, and beets all have little legs, and those legs are running so fast behind me. I look up and I can see Daddy's face in the window, and even though his plane is sputtering and making all sorts of noises, he is laughing at me being chased by those cans.

*I see his mouth move. He is saying, "Jump!
Jump, Amelia!" So I jump. And up I go. I jump
so high that I am as high as Daddy's plane. It
seems like nothing is moving, then, not his plane,
not me, not the cans. We are like a drawing on a
flat piece of paper. A silly drawing of a man in an
airplane with his mouth open wide from laughing,
and a girl who is just hanging in the air next to the
airplane, and on the ground, a bunch of cans with
arms and legs, standing around in a field, looking
up at us.*

I turned to a clean page in my memory book and
drew the picture that I saw in my dream. Then I
scribbled through it — something I hardly ever did
because I liked things to be neat. I drew it again and
this time I tore the page out of my notebook, trimmed
the raggedy edge, and hung it on the refrigerator.

On up in the morning, Mama went into town
with Brother Mustard Seed to buy a cane, as he wasn't
having much luck getting around on crutches. He'd

already broken one table lamp, and knocked the volume knob off the television set. He also mentioned he wanted to mail a letter off to his brother to give him directions to our house. He said his brother would be driving up from New Orleans in another week and a half.

While they were gone, Jerry Ray showed up with his tractor and the mowing machine and started cutting big swaths out of the weeds over in the runway field. I put Petey in the house because I was afraid he might go chasing after the tractor and get hit. I sat out on the front porch and watched Jerry Ray. There was something satisfying about watching those weeds come down.

In a few minutes I heard Petey making little yipping and growling noises inside the house. I looked through the screen door. Petey was standing in the middle of the living room floor with something in his mouth. I could see white stuffing on the carpet and the same white stuffing around his mouth.

"Petey! What are you doing? Drop it, Petey!" I yelled.

He dropped it, all right. There wasn't much left, but I could tell by the mangled thing that lay on the floor at Petey's feet what it had been. It was the Brother Mustard Seed doll. Its face was chewed up and wet from dog slobber. Its belly gaped open, and most of the cotton stuffing was scattered on the floor around it.

The next thing I remember I was standing on Miss Waters's front porch holding the doll in my hands with Petey yapping at my feet. I called through the screen, "Miss Waters! Are you home?"

Please be home, please be home, please be home, I was thinking. My tears fell into the open belly and soaked the cotton I'd tried to stuff back into the doll.

"Amelia, what's wrong?" Oshun threw open the screen door, grabbed me, and started hugging me all in one fast motion.

"Oshun? What are you doing here? You're not

supposed to be here!" Most of my words were choked off by the tears and her big hug. The doll was between us, and it was getting squashed by Oshun's big hug! I was crying more and trying to tell her to stop, but that just caused her to hug me even tighter. Finally, she loosened her grip and led me over to the porch swing.

"Don't tell me you've been crying like this ever since I've been gone! I tried to get you to go with me!"

"Oh, Oshun, I'm not crying over you. . . ." But then I saw that Oshun was grinning and had only been pulling my leg.

"Out with it, girl. What's going on and what's this thing? — oh, I know what it is — or WAS!"

"That's just it, Oshun. Petey chewed it up and . . ." I knew what I was about to tell Oshun was going to sound like I had lost my mind. But I had to tell her. Oshun would think of something to do to fix this mess. It's what friends are for.

I don't know how I was able to get the whole story out and have it make any kind of sense to her, especially since it didn't even make sense to me. But Oshun was a good listener, and she knew the right kind of questions to ask.

"First of all," she began after she'd heard the whole thing, "go dry your eyes and blow your nose — you're a mess. In fact, go to the bathroom and wash your face real good, then we'll get to the bottom of this. And if we can't, then we'll get Grandma to help us when she gets back from karate class."

Oshun was this way; she was a first-things-first sort of girl when she had to be, but most of the time she was an anything-goes girl. She held Petey in her lap and started picking the cotton stuffing out of his fur. "And just leave the doll out here," she said. She reached up and took it out of my hands.

The whole time I was in the bathroom I told myself over and over, *It's just a dumb doll. My mama's okay. Brother Mustard Seed's okay. It's just a dumb doll.*

I didn't cause them to have an accident. Everybody is going to be okay.

I walked back to the front porch with my face clean, but I wasn't feeling much better. Oshun was sitting there grinning like the cat that ate the mouse. She pointed over to my house with the Brother Mustard Seed doll.

"If that's the man you're so worried about, I think you can stop now. He looks like he's all in one piece, and even though I see a big gut, I don't see any of that big gut hanging out like this pitiful thing here. Your mama looks fine, too, except for whatever happened to her hair. Now there's an accident!"

Sure enough, Mama had just stepped out of the car and she looked okay. Brother Mustard Seed was looking up toward the house and calling for me. He didn't see me standing over on Miss Waters's porch.

"Amelia Forrest! Come look what we got here!" He waved his new cane around in the air above his head.

"What in the world is that stuff?" Oshun asked.

There was a flatbed trailer hooked to the back of Mama's car. On the trailer, in one big concrete pile, were lawn ornaments. I saw a couple of big concrete birds, and a medium-sized deer, which I'm sure was the one I saw on television the other night, because I recognized the stumpy little antlers. There were three or four turtles in different sizes, a couple with missing heads making it look like they'd pulled them inside their shells. I saw a lot of other pieces that looked like birdbaths, and maybe a few elves. At the back was a bear standing on its hind legs. It looked to be waving at any traffic that might have been following Mama and the trailer, but it was missing its paw.

Mama got out of the car and stood there for a minute looking at all those things. Except for her hair, she looked as gray as the pile of busted-up concrete lawn ornaments that she'd just hauled home.

"Let's go get a better look," Oshun said. She nudged Petey off her lap, then jumped off the porch and started across the yard. She still had the doll in her hand. She turned around and held it out to me. "You can either keep it and stitch it back up again, or you can let Petey have it as a chew toy. It doesn't make any difference, you know? Besides, I got us one that looks just like Pascal."

I'd let my imagination run away with me. No stupid doll had caused Brother Mustard Seed to fall off the ladder, and it wouldn't have caused any other accident, either. Things like that just didn't happen. It was good that Oshun was back to remind me that I was the sensible one. She was the one who did crazy things, who believed in impossible stuff, just for the fun of believing in it. *I keep my feet on the ground*, I was thinking to myself. Then I remembered what Miss Waters told me that Daddy had said one time: "That girl of mine has her head in the clouds, just like me, but her feet never leave the ground." I thought about my dream and the picture I drew. My feet were not on the ground in that picture.

"Let Petey have it," I told her. "It's too far gone."

"Come here, Petey," she called. She threw the doll to him, and as soon as he got it in his mouth he started shaking it and growling and throwing it around.

"You know, Amelia, it didn't even look like that man," Oshun said.

"It looked like him," I told her. "It was just a co-incidence, but it looked like him."

"Come on, I want to see him up close. I never met a born-again ex-convict before."

"How come you're back already?" I asked her. "I thought you were staying another month."

"Will and Maggie left Haiti and decided to go to Africa, to the Congo region. They said I could go with them or come back here. I think they're going to sleep in tents and eat insects or something. I said, 'No, thanks.' I'm glad I came back. This is a lot better."

This was a lot better? Was my summer turning out to be more exciting than Oshun's? My summer had been miserable so far. But it didn't seem that way to Oshun — she was seeing it as an adventure, and she couldn't wait to get over to my house to find out what was going to happen next.

And another thing: Will and Maggie? Hello? Since when did Oshun call her parents by their first names? And when did Miss Waters start taking karate classes? But I didn't get a chance to ask. Oshun was already halfway to my house, running, but stopping every once in a while to turn a cartwheel.

"hi, my name's Oshun Gregory."

I saw Brother Mustard Seed look up. Oshun had her hand out. He shifted around and tried to hold on to his cane and stick his hand out to shake hands with her all at the same time.

"Brother Mustard Seed here," he said. "Your name's Ocean? Like the sea? Like the Atlantic and that other one?"

Oshun laughed. "No, it's O-s-h-u-n, Oh-Shoon — like the goddess of sweet water and love."

"Forget it, Oshun," I told her. "Nobody's going to be impressed with that here."

"I'm a little impressed with it," said Brother Mustard Seed. "A name can be an important thing for a man — or a woman. I changed my name — used to be J. E. Abernathy."

"Yeah, Amelia told me. She said you are an ex-convict, that you stole a car, and . . ." I saw Brother

Mustard Seed gearing up for what was sure to be either a long story, a sermon, or possibly a heavy-duty crying jag.

By now, Mama was good at spotting this, too, and knew just what to do to turn his attention to something else. "Let's go inside and have a snack before we start unloading this stuff. I have to get the trailer back to that place before dark. And welcome back, Oshun. We want to hear about your trip, too."

"Yeah, well, my trip was boring compared to what's going on here. I want to know what all this stuff is for," Oshun said. "You've got some great things back there."

We all went inside the house. Oshun grabbed Brother Mustard Seed's left arm and helped him up the porch steps, as he wasn't doing such a hot job with the cane. In fact, I think he even whacked her across the shins with it once or twice.

Mama put out some pound cake and glasses of milk and asked Oshun about her trip to Haiti. Brother Mustard Seed asked if she'd seen any signs of voodoo stuff down there. Oshun got a twinkle in her eye, and I knew she was about to spill her guts about me and the Brother Mustard Seed doll. I kicked her under the table, which caused her to suck a piece of pound cake down the wrong way. She choked and Mama had to pat her on the back a couple of times until the cake came up, and she was all right again.

After that commotion, she kept her mouth shut about voodoo. Brother Mustard Seed looked ready to start talking about himself again — or at least about himself and the load of concrete misfits out on the flatbed trailer.

"You were right all along, Amelia Forrest. That's what your daddy meant, don't you see? When Brother Jed said, 'Go get them,' he wasn't talking about you and your mama. He meant the animals — just like you said."

"You think Daddy told you to bring home a load of broken concrete lawn ornaments?"

"Had to be. It was so easy. We drove into town, and your mama ran in to the post office to buy some stamps. I waited in the car and realized the concrete lawn ornament place was right across the street. The fellow I saw on TV that time, the one who owns the outfit, was hanging up a sign that said, 'Cheap.'"

"Meaning the busted-up ones?" I asked.

"Meaning the whole kit and caboodle. *Everything* he had was busted. An arm missing here, a head there, and so forth. *Everything*."

"Everything," Mama repeated.

"Well, I got out of the car and sauntered over there on my new cane that your mama bought for me, and I asked him, 'How much you want for your concrete pretties here?' And he said, 'Which one?' And I said, 'All of them.' Well, he looked a little surprised. He said, 'What you want 'em for?' And I said, 'I don't know. They're just kind of funny-looking.' So he told me if I'd haul 'em away I could have 'em."

"They're just kind of funny-looking?" I said. "That's why you wanted them?"

"Well, that and the fact that your daddy said, 'Go get them.' Plus the fact when you said, 'The concrete animals,' the idea just seemed to stick. But, yes, besides all that, when I really thought about it, I think I wanted them because they're funny-looking. I feel good when I look at them."

Oshun jumped in. "You probably don't know this, but my daddy's got just one leg. Do you think that's funny? Do you think people who are missing something are funny-looking?"

I couldn't believe what I was hearing. Number one, that Brother Mustard Seed bought a load of concrete creatures because he thought they were funny-looking; and number two, that Oshun was telling him that her daddy had just one leg, because he didn't — he had two legs.

"That's a lie, Oshun! Your daddy's got two legs like the rest of us!"

"Yeah, I know, but I was trying to make a point. It sounds like Brother Mustard Seed thinks that people who are different are 'funny-looking.' I just want to know what he means."

"That's a good question, Oshun. But I didn't say

anything about them being funny-looking because they're different. Maybe they just remind me that we're all missing something. Sometimes you can see what's missing — say, if somebody loses a leg, or a finger. But sometimes you can't tell when a person's missing something. Doesn't matter, though, the absence is there all the same."

"What's that got to do with being 'funny-looking'?" Oshun asked. She can be a real bulldog when she wants answers.

"Hmmmm. I don't guess I know. It's just that when I first saw that report on the news, I felt real sad. Then when I saw them there at that fellow's shop today, all lined up out front like they were waiting for somebody, I didn't feel sad anymore. I knew they were waiting for me. I knew right then that Brother Jed wanted me to get them and bring them home to Amelia and her mama."

I still didn't get it. I didn't think I'd ever get it. But, Oshun, who I guess felt her questions had been answered in a satisfactory manner by Brother Mustard Seed, seemed to be getting it. "We can paint them!" she cried. "They'll look great!"

"First we've got to unload them," Mama said. I realized then that she hadn't had too much to say about the concrete animals. What was she thinking? Was this part of the "change" that she thought would be good for us? Was she satisfied that when Daddy said "Go get them," he meant a load of concrete animals and not us?

"Come on, everybody up," she said, "I've got to get that trailer back to town before that place closes. Amelia, you and Oshun go out and start unloading the light ones. I'll straighten up in here, then I'll be on out to help unload the heavy stuff in a minute."

Brother Mustard Seed, with his broken foot, wasn't much help. Basically, he stood to the side and told us what to do. Oshun and I each picked up a concrete bird. Hers was missing its beak. Mine had a crack down the middle but still had all its parts. They were heavier than you might have imagined. We set them down on the edge of the driveway, next to the trailer.

"Where are we going to put them — I mean, for good?" I asked. I couldn't imagine that Mama would want them all over the front yard. She had flowers and stuff growing everywhere now and was kind of picky about how it looked.

Brother Mustard Seed looked out over Daddy's newly mowed landing strip. He started pointing his cane. "There," he said. "And there," he pointed again. "And there and there and there and there!"

I felt a tight knot start to form at the back of my throat. "No," I said. "We can't put them there." I felt like I might choke. I had to put down the concrete elf I was holding. "I have to keep the runway clear," I said. "I'm supposed to keep it clear. That's what Daddy told me to do."

Oshun looked at me. "Are you okay?"

Was I losing my mind or what? I felt as busted apart as that stupid concrete pile of rubble. Missing something. Like Brother Mustard Seed had told Oshun. We were all missing something.

"I'm sorry, Amelia. We don't have to put them there. Let's just set them down here at the edge of the yard for now," Brother Mustard Seed said.

"Oh, forget it. I guess it doesn't matter where we put them. It's just a regular old field now, anyway."

About that time, Mama walked up. "Did I hear you right? 'It's just a field,' Amelia?"

"Brother Mustard Seed wants us to put the concrete lawn ornaments out there," Oshun told her. "And tomorrow we get to paint them!"

"Out there?" Mama asked. "On Jed's landing strip?"

That's when Brother Mustard Seed leaned in close and whispered in my ear, "It's what your daddy wants, Amelia. I can prove it, too. Look at this." Brother Mustard Seed reached into the pocket of his pants and pulled out a folded piece of notebook paper. He opened it up for me to see. It was the drawing

I had made of my dream. Up in the sky was an airplane with a man inside just laughing to beat the band. Next to the plane, hanging there in the air, was a girl — me — looking surprised. And down below were dozens of cans, or concrete lawn ornaments, or something, scattered out over the field.

when I opened my eyes in the middle of the night and had goose bumps running up and down my spine, the first thing I always thought was that maybe there was a crazed person hiding in the shadows of my room, or under my bed. But then I would get hold of myself and think, *It was probably just a nightmare*.

But sometimes goose bumps in the middle of the night meant something else. Sometimes they meant that something big had happened the day before but I couldn't remember what. I had to just lie there in bed and go over the day in my head until I came to it again. Oh, yeah, I remembered.

I walked over to the window and looked out. From my bedroom I could see most of the runway. The night was clear, and there was enough moonlight that I could see the concrete lawn ornaments scattered all up and down the runway. My shoulders were sore from lugging those things around. We hadn't put them in a straight line or anything. Brother Mustard Seed had told us where to put them, and they were not in any kind of order at all. There was a turtle. Next to it was a Dutch boy. Several feet away there was a concrete fox missing its ear. Altogether there were twenty-five pieces. They looked white, ghostly white out there against the dark ground.

Then I saw one of them move! One of the figures moved away from the others! It reached out and touched the tall bear missing its paw. I saw then that it was Mama and not one of the concrete animals. The moonlight reflected off her red curls, leaving me no doubt that it was her.

She looked lonely standing down there in the middle of that big mess. She had been going along with whatever Brother Mustard Seed told her. Wanting so much to believe that Daddy was trying to tell us something. Willing to believe anything — even that unloading twenty-five busted-up concrete lawn ornaments onto an open field and then painting them was the thing to do. The thing that Daddy wanted us to do. I tiptoed out of the house to be with her. It didn't feel right to leave her all alone out in the middle of those heavy, silent creatures.

"Mama," I said softly. It was so quiet out there. My voice seemed too loud, too human, or something.

"Amelia, what are you doing up? It's the middle of the night."

"I know, Mama, but I woke up and I saw you out here. At first I thought you were one of them."

"One of them?" she asked.

"One of the concrete things," I said. "And then I saw you move!"

Mama laughed a little bit and then she said, "With everything else that's been happening, would that be so strange?"

"No, I guess not," I said. We sat down together. The field was damp with dew, and I knew that our nightgowns would be soaked through. It didn't look like Mama cared, so I decided not to care, either. "Mama, what *is* happening?"

"Hmmm, good question. Let's see, what *is*

happening? Well, we have a man in our basement — a man just out of prison — who says he can see your daddy. Not only can *see* him, but can *hear* him as well. And we've got concrete lawn ornaments out here where your daddy used to land his airplane."

"It's weird, isn't it, Mama? Remember how Daddy was about his field? Remember how I always kept the sticks and stuff picked up for him? It was my job. And now look at it."

I couldn't hold it in anymore. I started crying, and Mama was crying, too. We must have looked a strange sight sitting out there in our nightgowns, crying our eyes out in between a concrete reindeer and a concrete poodle.

"Oh, Amelia. It's not your job anymore. Do you understand?"

I wiped my nose with the back of my hand. From somewhere in the folds of her gown, Mama came up with a tissue.

"I was supposed to take care of things," I spluttered. "In the note that Daddy left, he wrote, 'Keep the runway clear.' That meant take care of things. I haven't been taking care of anything. Everything's a mess. I don't even know what to do to fix things!"

"Maybe that's what Daddy's trying to tell you now, Amelia. That you don't have to fix things. That there's no need to keep the runway clear. Maybe he's showing you that by covering it with all these heavy things."

We sat there in the middle of all that concrete and quiet. Mama had her arm around me. I saw that we were facing the direction that Daddy would fly in when he landed the plane.

"Mama, I want to tell you something. A secret, something I've been keeping a secret ever since that day."

"What are you talking about, Amelia? What secret? What day?"

"I think I might have caused Daddy to crash the plane. I think it was my fault."

"Amelia, you didn't cause the crash. Nobody knows what caused it."

"You're not listening. That morning, when Daddy

was getting ready to leave, I watched him from my bedroom window. I saw him go over to Miss Waters's house to pick up something, and that's when I sneaked out . . ."

"Go on, Amelia, tell me what happened."

"Remember that little green popping monster that Daddy scared me with the night before? Well, I put it in his plane, down on the floor behind his seat, and I set it to go off. It must have popped when he was flying over that mountain. I think it scared him, and he lost control and crashed."

Mama hugged me to her. She wasn't saying anything. I didn't know how she felt. I didn't know how I felt about telling her. I had thought it might feel good to get it off my chest, but I didn't feel anything so far — just sad like before.

"Amelia, your daddy was an excellent pilot — the best. Do you think something like that would be enough to shake him? You think that would be enough to make him lose control of the plane? He was trained for anything, Amelia. The crash was not your fault."

"You don't know that, Mama. Not for sure. I tried to tell myself the same thing when it first happened. But I remember Daddy told me that flying takes a pilot's full concentration, how you couldn't afford to be distracted by anything. It could have happened, Mama."

"No, Amelia, the investigators came to no conclusion about the crash. You know what they said — 'a crash of undetermined origin.'"

"That's just because they didn't know about the popper. But it could have happened that way, Mama. You may as well admit it. Go on and say it."

"No, Amelia. I won't."

Nobody said anything for a few minutes. I realized that it didn't matter, anyway. If Mama didn't want to believe that I could have caused the crash, then she didn't have to. I was the one who would have to live with it for the rest of my life.

"You should have said something about this sooner, Amelia. You should have told me that this is what you've been thinking all this time."

"Sometimes I wanted to. I tried in the beginning,

but it seemed like it would just hurt you more. Then later I just wanted to forget about it."

"Amelia, you can't go through your life thinking you were responsible for that crash. Nobody knows what happened, and never will. It was an accident, and you have to accept it as that."

"I wish I could believe it, but the hard fact is, there's no way I can be sure."

"Amelia, you and that monster popper toy had absolutely nothing to do with your daddy's plane crash, and that's the truth. That's all I have to know, and that's all you have to know."

I didn't say anything. There wasn't anything left to say. I had told her everything. I guess I felt a little bit better, like maybe I wasn't carrying the whole thing by myself anymore. That was worth something. And I guess in a way it all came down to what you *want* to believe, anyway, which was what Mama had said before. You choose what you want to believe and what you don't want to believe. Mama didn't want to believe that I was responsible for the crash, so she was choosing not to believe it, and that was that.

"Mama, you know what I said about running away? I wouldn't do that to you for anything in the world. I'm sorry for saying it and worrying you. And I'm sorry, too, for smarting off so much about everything. I mean it. I'm still not sure how I feel about all this Brother Mustard Seed business, but I know that no matter what, Daddy would want us to stay together. I love you, Mama."

She pulled me up close to her, and I realized that the chemical smell around her head had finally gone away.

"Back at you, Amelia Forrest. I love you, too."

"I miss him, Mama. I miss Daddy so much sometimes, I can't stand it."

"I do, too," she said. "I miss him every day."

"You know what people say when somebody dies, how that person is always alive to you as long as you have your memories? It's not true. I've even got a memory book where I write things down. But it's not the same as having him here. It's not the same at all."

"I know that, Amelia."

We sat out there awhile longer. Talking a little about this and that — but not about the crash. We even laughed and said how silly we must have looked out in the field in the middle of the night. I told Mama about the Brother Mustard Seed doll and how at first I thought I might have caused him to fall off the ladder.

"The man was standing on a metal ladder in sock feet, stapling into live Christmas lights!" Mama said. And the way she said it, we both started laughing so hard that we had tears in our eyes again. Not because he got hurt, but because we couldn't believe he'd done such a thing.

"And then this morning when you went to town, I found Petey chewing the doll to pieces," I told her. "The stuffing was all over the living room floor like guts, and I ran screaming over to Miss Waters's house!"

Well, I guess Mama thought this was the funniest

thing she'd ever heard. And all of a sudden, it did seem funny. I laughed so hard that my stomach ached, but I didn't want to stop. I couldn't remember the last time we had laughed so hard.

We settled down a little, then, and wiped our eyes with another tissue that Mama pulled out of a pocket.

"Do you still think Brother Mustard Seed's a — let me think of some of the names you've called him — a creep? A lunatic? A freeloader? A kook?" Mama asked me.

I had been really mean to that man. He wanted so much to help us. He honestly thought he was doing what Daddy had asked him to do. Despite the faces I made at him, the names I called him, the hateful words I slung at him, he still liked me, still accepted me just as I am, the same as Daddy had done for him.

"To tell you the truth, Mama, I don't know what to think about him. He's a little out of the ordinary, like you said. But I can see why Daddy liked him. I guess I can even see why Daddy would appear to him, I mean if he was going to appear to anybody. It's so easy for Brother Mustard Seed to believe — he simply *believes*, no questions asked. Daddy knew that about him."

"You're right, Amelia. In his own way, I think Daddy's still watching out for us. Look at all these concrete guardians he's sent us!"

I looked around at all the animals, boys, girls, and elves that we were sitting in the middle of. "It's funny, Mama, but they all look like they're smiling, every one of them. Did you notice that before?"

"You're right," she said. "They do look like they're smiling — at least the ones with heads."

That set us off again, and it was four o'clock in the morning before we finally went back to bed. My gown was sopping wet from sitting out there in the field, and I had grass cuttings sticking to the backs of my legs. But I didn't care.

I fell asleep immediately. I didn't wake up until noon the next day. The first thing I did was look out the window and make sure the lawn ornaments were still there — that it hadn't all been a dream.

It wasn't a dream. Oshun was down there with a wheelbarrow full of open paint cans.

"Hey!" I called down to her. "What are you doing?"

"Well, looky there, Miss Sleeping Beauty wakes up!"

Brother Mustard Seed was sitting in a lawn chair next to a bright red turtle. His broken foot was propped up on a nearby concrete raccoon. He had a brush in his hand and was painting yellow stars on the red turtle's back. Waving his other hand, he yelled up to me, "Yeah, Sleeping Beauty, why don't you come down and join the paint party!" Petey sat next to Brother Mustard Seed's broken foot like he was guarding it or something.

"Where's Mama?" I asked. I figured she might be sleeping, though not for long with all the hollering that was going on.

"She went into town with Grandma. They went to get more paint — we need green," yelled Oshun.

"And purple, I asked for purple," Brother Mustard Seed added.

At first I wanted to say how stupid it was going to look to have all those painted things out in our field. But would it really look stupid? And if it did look stupid, would it matter? Who would care? It was our field. It used to be a landing strip, but it wasn't a landing strip anymore, it was a field. Daddy wasn't coming back. I could keep the runway clear, but it wouldn't matter.

And then I missed Daddy like I had never missed him before. I missed him so much and so hard that it hurt. My ribs and stomach were sore from hauling those heavy concrete things all over the field, and also from laughing hard with Mama last night, and that's where it felt like I missed him the most. I started crying just as hard as I had laughed with Mama. It felt like something was going to break loose inside me. I closed the window and sat down on the floor. I was glad nobody was in the house to hear me. It was the kind of crying that could only come out when you were alone. I cried until it seemed like there was nothing left inside me but a raw, empty place.

My memory book was on the table next to my bed. I flipped it open to the page where I had pasted Daddy's note. I read: *P.S. You are no NERVOUS NELLIE. You're my brave Amelia, and I love you very much.*

I touched the word "brave." Had I been brave? I didn't feel brave. I felt scared and nervous — especially when things happened that I didn't expect to happen.

This whole business with Brother Mustard Seed was not what I had expected for my summer of improvement. I walked over to the window and looked down again. I stood to the side, where they couldn't see me if they looked up. Oshun had started painting the raccoon orange. Their voices carried up to my window. I heard Brother Mustard Seed say, "Paint my broken foot, Oshun!"

I looked back at the note. I didn't really know what brave meant. Soldiers were brave in battle. People who rescued other people were brave. But what did that have to do with me? Did it have anything to do with letting my feet leave the ground? Miss Waters said you had to do that every once in a while.

Did it mean that sometimes you had to do something without really knowing the full reason for doing it? For instance, if I went down and painted a concrete animal, would that be a way of being brave? *Who knows?* I told myself, but I decided it would beat sitting around in my room all day crying my eyes out. I was pretty sure that was not what Daddy would have wanted.

I looked back at Daddy's note to me and traced my finger under his words *I love you very much.*

"Back at you, Daddy," I said out loud in the quiet room.

When I got down there, Oshun handed me a paintbrush. "You're going to have the coolest field of anybody!"

I grabbed a paintbrush and a can of silver paint. I started on the concrete bear standing on its hind legs. I decided to give it a silver head. Maybe it would look a little like an astronaut wearing a helmet.

The sun was hot. Brother Mustard Seed's face was redder than usual, especially considering that he wasn't crying.

"Amelia, have you seen my cap? I remember I wore it that first day I came walking up here. Your daddy gave me that cap once when he came to visit. He was wearing it and, when I admired it, he said, 'It's yours, then.' He was like that."

So that had been Daddy's cap? Come to think of it, maybe I had seen a picture of Daddy wearing that PRAY HARD cap and holding me when I was a little baby. I remembered when Brother Mustard Seed first showed up on the front porch wearing it, I had gotten the strangest feeling that things wouldn't be the same. I was right: Things hadn't been the same.

"I surely believe I'm going to need a cap or

something. I've got what you might call delicate skin. I don't want to burn."

"I'll find your cap," I told him. If I remembered right, I had stuck it behind a pot of geraniums on the front porch. I didn't know why I did it — it just seemed like the thing to do at the time. Funny he hadn't asked for it before now, but when I thought about it, he hadn't really spent much time outside since he'd been here. He was more of an indoor kind of guy.

But his cap was not behind the geraniums. I looked in the house. I went down to the basement, thinking that maybe he'd found it and put it with the rest of his stuff. But I couldn't find it anywhere.

The only other place to look was under the porch. Petey was bad about dragging stuff under there. I hoped that wasn't where it was. I didn't like to crawl back in that dark, damp place.

I pushed the loose board back and peeked in. The light showed through the cracks in the porch floor and made thin white slivers, like stripes, on the packed dirt. It smelled like dirt and wet dog under there.

Wouldn't you know it? I saw that red cap, along with a bunch of other stuff back about as far as you could go. There was no way I could reach it with my arm. I would have to crawl in on my hands and knees. I wondered why Petey liked to hide stuff, wondered if I should break him of the habit or just nail up the loose board.

I got the hat, and it didn't seem to be chewed up too bad. Under the hat was what was left of the Brother Mustard Seed doll. Next to that was a sandal that I thought I'd lost last summer. And then I saw something else — something green. I picked it up and held it in my hands.

The green monster popper.

I backed out of the space and sat on the ground. I looked at the thing like I thought it might tell me what had happened. The spring was a little rusty, and Petey had chewed off one of the suction cups.

Had Daddy found it before he left that morning

and thrown it out? Had Petey climbed up into Daddy's plane and found it? What did it mean, anyway? That the crash wasn't my fault?

Mama and Miss Waters drove up around that time. I walked out to the car to meet them, holding the tiny toy in one hand and the cap in the other.

"Come on over here, Amelia, help us with this paint," Mama called to me.

I held the toy out. "Look what I found, Mama. It was under the porch with Petey's stuff."

"The popper! Oh, Amelia, I told you. I told you."

About that time, Miss Waters walked over and saw what I was holding. "Where'd you find that, Amelia?" she asked.

"It was under the porch, Miss Waters. The last morning that Daddy left I set it to go off in his plane. It was supposed to be a joke. I wanted to get him back for scaring me with it. I thought it went off while he was flying over that mountain. I thought it was what caused Daddy to crash."

"You thought you caused the crash — with that little toy there? All this time you've been thinking that, Amelia?" Her eyebrows seemed even higher than usual, making her look more surprised than ever.

Then she grabbed me and hugged me up to her so tight. She had a big hug like Oshun's — the kind where you feel hugged all over, not just your neck or your back.

"Let me tell you something about that morning," she said. "Your daddy walked over to pick up a package I had put together for the flood victims. I was sitting on the porch having some coffee, and he came over and we talked for a few minutes. Then he picked up the box and walked back to the plane. I looked down and noticed a couple of cans and whatnot that I had forgotten to put in the box. So I hurried over there to give them to him before he left. He was sitting in his seat, the door was still open, and he was checking over his instruments. The plane was running, and I had to shout to be heard.

"'Jed,' I said, 'here's a few more things!' He reached down and took them from me. Then, *pop!* We heard a noise, a loud pop and a whistle. Well, your daddy started laughing and shaking his head. He reached down and picked that little toy up off the floor. 'That Amelia,' he said. 'She told me she'd get me back. Hang on to this for me, Miss Waters. I'll fix her wagon tonight!'

"I took the toy and went on back to the porch and sat down. I forgot all about it until we got the news about what had happened. I'd left the toy out on the porch that morning. When I went to look for it, it was gone. I figured Petey had carried it off. I had no idea you'd been thinking about that little thing all this time, Amelia. I wish I'd said something."

"It's okay, Miss Waters. You didn't know. I almost told you once, but I just couldn't do it."

"She didn't tell me, either," Mama said. "Not until last night. We got a lot of talking done last night, didn't we, Amelia?"

About that time, Brother Mustard Seed hobbled

over on his cane. "You found my cap! That's my lucky cap!"

"It was under the porch," I told him. "It's got a little dog slobber on it, but not much."

"I don't care," he said. "It'll keep the sun off just the same. Come on, let's paint. Did you get the purple?"

"Purple, green, and a shade I picked out called Bird's Egg Blue," Miss Waters told him.

"I thought you were allergic to paint," I said.

"Oh, you bet I am, Amelia Forrest. But it's usually not bad if I'm outdoors. If I get to wheezing, I'll quit painting."

Oshun was working hard on the raccoon. It was orange, and she was painting yellow zigzags of lightning on it.

"I made a pitcher of lemonade," Mama said. "I'll run in and get it. We need to cool off a little before we get started."

"I'll get it, Mama," I told her. I wanted to take the toy inside and put it somewhere safe. I didn't want to wake up tomorrow morning and start thinking that maybe I hadn't really found it.

I put the green monster popper on the table next to my bed. It's where Daddy had put it that last night to show me that it wasn't spring-loaded, and that there was no danger of it going off.

Then I went to the refrigerator to get the lemonade. My drawing was there. Brother Mustard Seed had unfolded it and tried to smooth the creases out of it. It was a funny-looking thing, and it made me feel good to look at it — just like Brother Mustard Seed had said about the busted-up lawn ornaments.

"It's a great picture, Amelia," Mama said from behind me. "It's just the kind of . . ." And then I don't know what she was going to say next because she was interrupted by a loud holler from outside.

Brother Mustard Seed was yelling, "BIRDS!" at the top of his lungs.

We ran out onto the porch. A big, dark cloud of birds was coming in. Some landed on the grass in the field, and some perched on top of the concrete statues.

"The ravens," I said.

"Tricksters! Jokers! Seekers of Secrets!" Brother Mustard called out everything he remembered from the encyclopedia.

The birds were noisy. Just like before, they screeched and croaked.

"They're laughing!" Oshun said. "You think they're laughing at us? At what we're doing?"

"They're not laughing," I told her. "They're making some kind of weird bird sound, but they're not laughing."

"Oh, it sounds like laughing to me," said Mama.

"It's laughing, all right," Miss Waters said.

"Yes-sir-ee, they're laughing," said Brother Mustard Seed. "But they're not laughing at us, they're laughing with us."

Until he said that, nobody had been laughing — but then we were, all of us — people and birds alike.

Then, as if they'd gotten a signal from some-where, they all lifted up at the same time and flew off, leaving us standing there in the middle of those busted and cracked lawn ornaments.

Had the birds been laughing at us? Were they laughing *with* us, like Brother Mustard Seed said? I re-membered what Daddy had said about the birds laughing at him for trying so hard to be like them — for trying to fly.

I looked at Brother Mustard Seed standing there with his shoe freshly painted orange. I saw that Oshun had written GET WELL in green paint on the side of his soft cast. Or maybe he had written it on there himself, which wouldn't have surprised me at all. I wondered if the visions were over. I wondered if he'd even had one in the first place, or was it just him thinking about Daddy — thinking about a good friend he hadn't heard from in a long time?

My best friend, Oshun, had three green stripes on her face that I was sure she had put there herself. She was already back to work on the orange raccoon with lightning bolts down its side, making it look something like a race car.

Mama was trying to pry open the can of purple paint for Brother Mustard Seed. He was standing over her with his paintbrush in one hand and his cane in the other, trying to tell her the best way to open the can. "Hold your horses," she said to him. "I know what I'm doing." Her red curls blazed even redder in the noonday sun, almost matching the red PRAY HARD cap that protected Brother Mustard Seed's delicate head.

When I looked at Miss Waters I saw that she had been watching me, for how long, I don't know. "She's got a special way of seeing things," Oshun had always said.

She handed me my paintbrush and winked. "Amelia Forrest, you got your head in the clouds or something?"

I laughed. "Do you think that's something I could do and keep my feet on the ground at the same time?"

"No, girl. Not all the time. Most of the time, sure.

But look at you. You've been laughing with birds and now you're getting ready to paint a big ol' concrete bear with silver paint. You know what your daddy would say about that?"

"What?" I asked.

"That your feet just left the ground."